The Bible Activity Book

The Bible Activity Book

Packed with games, puzzles, mazes
and activities that will bring your
best-loved Bible stories to life

ARCTURUS

This edition published in 2010 by Arcturus Publishing Limited
26/27 Bickels Yard, 151–153 Bermondsey Street,
London SE1 3HA

ISBN: 978-1-84837-588-8
CH001397EN

Written by Helen Otway
Design and illustration by Dynamo Limited
Edited by Anna Brett

Printed in Singapore

God's Busy Week

God spent six days creating all the wonderful things on Earth. Can you spot eight differences between these two scenes showing life on Earth at the end of the first week?

Colourful Creations

Use your pens or pencils to make God's creations bright and beautiful!

Which World?

All these pictures of God's Earth look the same, but can you spot which one is slightly different from the others?

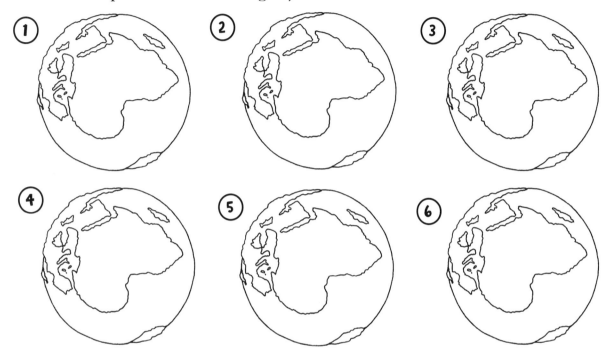

Wonderful Work

God worked hard to build up our world one step at a time. Using a pencil, see if you can match up these days with what God created on each one.

First day	God rested
Second day	Sun, moon and stars
Third day	Light and darkness
Fourth day	Animals and humans
Fifth day	Land and sea
Sixth day	Birds and sea creatures
Seventh day	Sky

One World

On the seventh day God had finished creating Earth and it was ready for all to enjoy! Can you find your way through the maze to reach it?

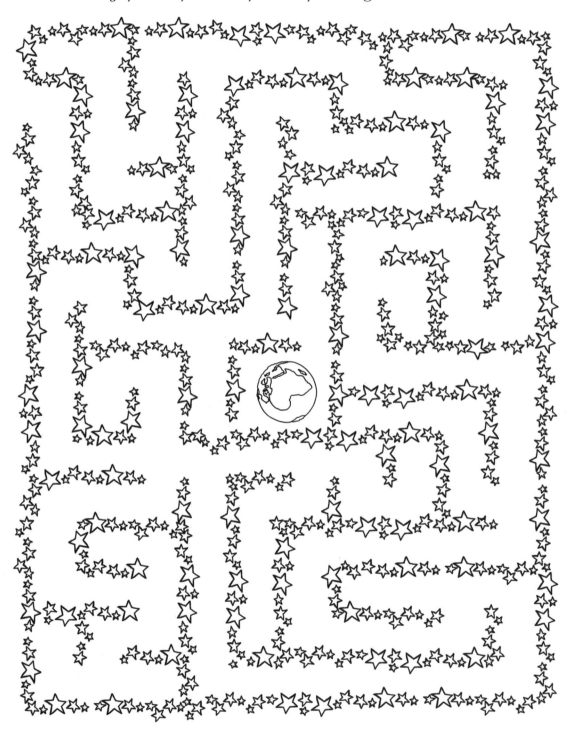

Creation Search

Can you find these words from the Creation story hidden in this wordsearch square? The words read forwards, backwards, up, down and diagonally.

```
F  P  C  P  E  O  P  L  E  S  R  A  T  S  O
D  V  Y  G  C  P  V  T  T  Y  F  K  D  O  G
J  M  A  E  F  D  Q  Q  H  E  K  P  Z  O  D
J  A  A  A  N  O  W  Y  S  G  U  S  J  Y  I
J  N  D  E  U  Q  R  E  M  I  Y  R  Y  H
Y  J  N  C  Q  F  E  P  M  C  Y  L  L  R  T
J  S  N  J  R  V  E  A  R  T  H  W  T  Y  B
X  N  W  L  I  E  A  E  K  F  I  F  X  W  L
E  N  T  N  D  T  A  I  D  X  K  U  I  V  W
A  L  U  E  D  T  N  T  D  N  Z  I  T  X  B
W  Z  K  P  O  O  A  N  I  M  A  L  S  I  F
M  R  J  R  O  J  Z  N  B  O  M  S  S  I  H
E  S  I  M  S  D  D  H  W  S  N  K  M  I  D
Y  B  X  Y  V  D  M  Y  U  P  I  B  H  H  N
B  E  G  I  N  N  I  N  G  X  S  L  A  N  D
```

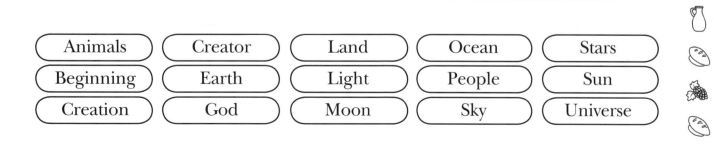

Animals	Creator	Land	Ocean	Stars
Beginning	Earth	Light	People	Sun
Creation	God	Moon	Sky	Universe

Adam And Eve

God made a beautiful garden for Adam and Eve to live in. Can you find eight differences between these two pictures of the Garden of Eden?

The Garden Of Eden

The Garden of Eden was bursting with pretty flowers and tasty fruit for Adam and Eve to enjoy! Study this picture for 20 seconds and then turn the page to answer some questions about it.

Question Time

Now you've studied the picture of God's special garden on page 11, try to answer these questions without peeking!

1. Which animal appears in the picture?
2. Who is the woman in the picture?
3. Who is holding an apple?
4. How many apples are there on the tree?
5. Did you spot how many leaves there are on the tree?
6. How many flowers are there in the garden?
7. Who is the man in the picture?

Bonus question: What is the garden they are in called?
a) Paradise b) Eden c) Tranquillity

Forbidden Fruit

God told Adam and Eve that there was only one tree they shouldn't eat from, but this sly snake is hoping to trick them. Which path should he slither along to reach the apple tree?

Temptation Wordsearch

Can you find these words from the Adam and Eve story hidden in the wordsearch? The words read forwards, backwards, up, down and diagonally.

```
            S   I   N
        Q   V   G   S   X   T   F
      U   F   A   J   N   L   E   I   A
    A   I   R   E   N   A   O   M   R   S   R
  V   E   D   S   M   M   K   N   P   S   T   I   H
  A   E   N   N   W   C   E   D   T   T   X   B   R
X   N   T   L   A   M   D   T   J   A   M   V   L   T   S
E   M   O   N   K   E   R   T   E   T   A   X   R   D   F
T   V   R   X   E   U   N   L   I   I   N   E   Y   X   S
J   E   I   X   P   P   F   T   O   E   E   D   T
L   C   S   N   P   R   G   J   N   B   P   I   D
  G   H   A   U   A   E   X   O   I   U   O
    O   N   X   X   X   S   O   R   O
        D   E   U   I   Z   F   N
            D   F   G
```

Adam	Eden	Fruit	Rib	Snake
Apple	Eve	Garden	Serpent	Temptation
Disobey	First man	God	Sin	Tree

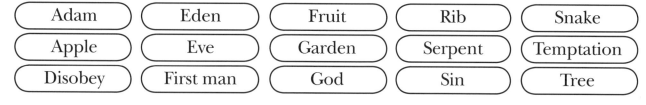

Slippery Serpent

Only one of these is the snake that persuaded Eve to eat a forbidden apple.
He is different from the rest – can you spot which one he is?

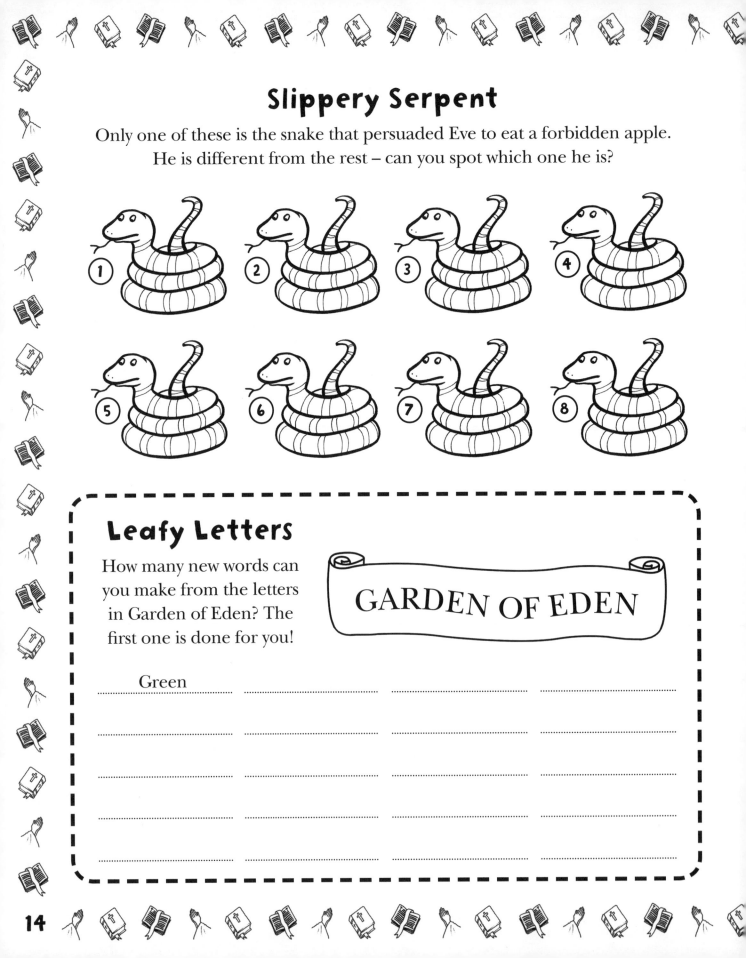

Leafy Letters

How many new words can you make from the letters in Garden of Eden? The first one is done for you!

GARDEN OF EDEN

Green

Flood Alert

God warned Noah that a huge flood was on its way. Can you spot the eight differences between these two pictures of Noah building an ark for his family?

Water World

Once the Earth was flooded, Noah set sail with his family and two of all God's creatures. Which piece completes this picture of Noah and his amazing ark?

Two By Two

Noah agreed to take a pair of every animal on his ark, so it was a pretty noisy place! Look carefully at this picture for 20 seconds and then turn the page to answer the questions. You can colour in the picture too!

All About The Ark

Now you've studied the picture of Noah's ark on page 17, see how much you can remember without looking back!

1. How many levels does the ark have?
2. How many portholes are there?
3. How many different types of animal are there?
4. Which animal is swinging from the top floor?
5. What is Noah's wife feeding the horse?
6. Which animal is eating hay?
7. Which animal is in the pen?

Bonus question: How long did it rain for?
a) Four days and four nights. b) Forty days and forty nights. c) A whole year.

Land Ahoy!

Noah sent a dove to see if the floodwaters were draining away.
Which path did it follow to find an olive tree to perch on?

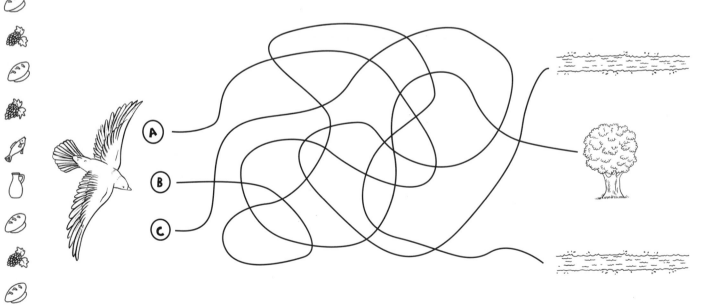

On Dry Land

When the water had drained away, Noah and the animals could leave the ark! Can you show which way the ark sailed to find dry land?

Looking For Land

Can you find these words from the story of Noah hidden in this wordsearch?
The words read forwards, backwards, up, down and diagonally.

```
C  E  L  M  O  U  N  T  A  I  N  A  N  G  P
N  A  R  K  Y  X  N  O  J  M  A  E  C  H  J
N  Q  X  X  A  K  B  Z  V  I  W  C  A  U  E
K  R  A  Z  N  S  E  R  U  T  A  E  R  C  Z
R  A  I  N  I  N  G  U  E  M  I  H  P  R  Q
F  P  T  N  M  Y  I  K  V  T  N  N  E  O  D
C  F  M  W  A  R  J  V  O  R  A  A  N  P  N
V  O  K  Z  L  T  J  U  D  F  Q  W  T  S  O
Y  R  F  D  S  A  P  R  D  U  S  F  E  E  A
O  T  T  O  T  O  B  O  J  N  C  E  R  F  H
B  Y  O  O  C  B  S  B  Q  P  A  X  E  I  S
H  D  L  L  R  E  Q  R  K  P  D  L  F  L  Y
B  A  P  F  M  T  A  D  I  R  N  N  I  W  A
L  Y  F  G  W  S  F  N  E  A  X  N  L  E  D
J  S  F  N  Q  R  A  F  L  H  P  D  S  N  U
```

Animals	Creatures	Land	Pairs
Ark	Dove	Mountain	Raining
Boat	Flood	New life	Ocean
Carpenter	Forty days	Noah	Water

 20

What's The Story?

Look carefully at this picture to see what is happening. Do you know which bible story it comes from? It tells of how people built the T _ _ _ _ of B _ _ _ _ to try and reach up to heaven.

Tower Tour

These men have heard about the great tower and are coming to have a look! Which way should they go to reach it?

Men At Work

Many men worked hard to build their tower – they had to bake their own bricks in those days, too! Can you spot eight differences between the two pictures?

Tower Tools

While the tower was being built, God decided that the people should speak different languages. These five men are looking for their hammers but no one can understand each other! Can you locate all ten hammers?

Sky Scraper

The Tower of Babel got so tall that its top went right through the clouds! Which piece completes this picture of the tower to the sky?

Waiting For God

Abraham was an ordinary man before God paid him a visit! Use your favourite pens and pencils to colour this picture of Abraham at sunset.

Which Way To Canaan?

Abraham trusted in God and left everything behind to move to the town called Canaan. Which path did he follow to get there?

Hush Little Baby

Baby Isaac is crying for his mum and dad, Sarah and Abraham. Which way should they go to comfort him?

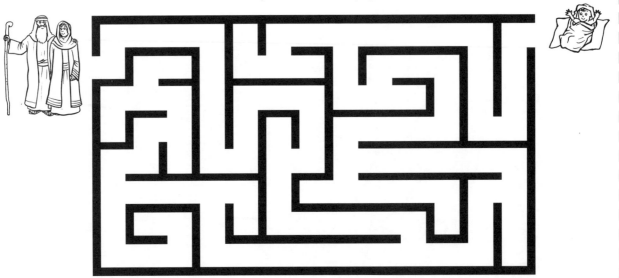

A New Baby

God blessed Abraham and his wife Sarah with a sweet baby son. Which piece completes this picture of Abraham, Sarah and baby Isaac?

A Precious Son

God tested Abraham by asking him to give up his only son. Use your pens or pencils to colour this picture of Abraham with Isaac.

Eyes On Isaac

These pictures of Isaac all look the same, but one is different from the others. Can you spot which one?

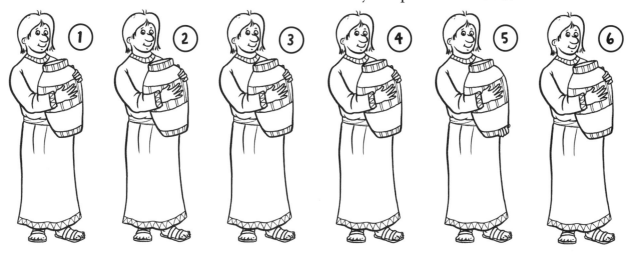

Abraham's Test

Can you fill in these blanks to complete the facts about the story of Abraham and Isaac?

1. God wanted to teach A _ _ _ _ _ _ that human
   s _ _ _ _ _ _ _ _ _ were wrong.

2. G_ _ also wanted to see how l _ _ _ _ Abraham was to his commands.

3. Abraham was ordered to sacrifice his son I _ _ _ _ to God.

4. Isaac and Abraham travelled for t _ _ _ _ days to the
   m _ _ _ _ _ _ _ God had chosen.

5. Just as Abraham was about to sacrifice Isaac, an a _ _ _ _ came
   down and told him it was a t _ _ _ from God.

Isaac And Rebekah

Abraham sent a servant back to his homeland to find a beautiful wife for his son.
Which piece completes this picture of Isaac meeting Rebekah?

A   B   C   D

Marriage Maze

Which way should Isaac go to ask Rebekah to marry him?

Well, Well!

Abraham's servant met Rebekah by a well, when she kindly offered him and his camels a drink. Which of these wells is different from the others?

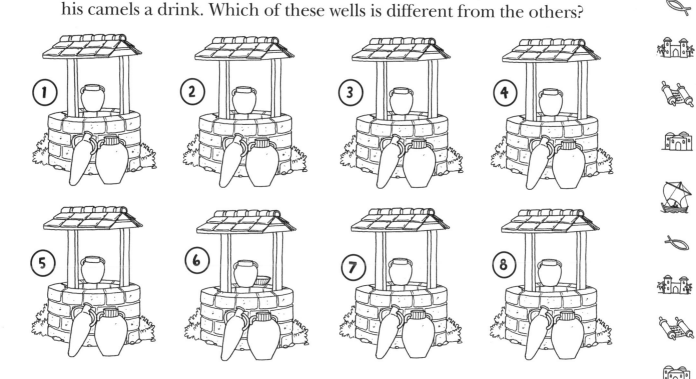

Jacob's Dream

Look carefully at this picture. Do you know the story that it comes from? The story tells of Jacob's amazing dream about a l_ _ _ _ _ that led up to h _ _ _ _ _ .

Awesome Angels

Jacob saw angels drifting up and down the steps in his dream. Which of these angels is about to travel up the ladder to heaven?

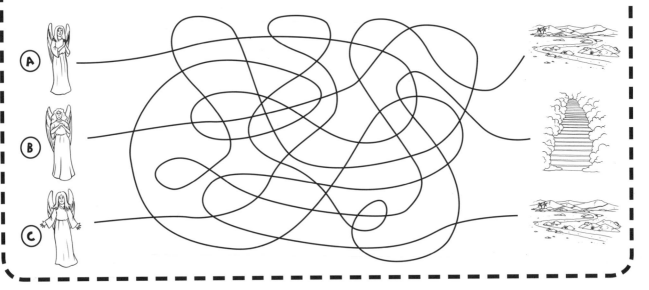

God Bless

In Jacob's dream, God promised that he would always watch over him. Use your pencils or pens to colour the picture of dreaming Jacob using the key below.

(1) Red (2) Green (3) Brown (4) Blue
(5) Yellow (6) Orange (7) Pink

Lucky Joseph

Jacob had twelve sons, but Joseph was extra special to him. Which way did Jacob go to give a smart new robe to his favourite son?

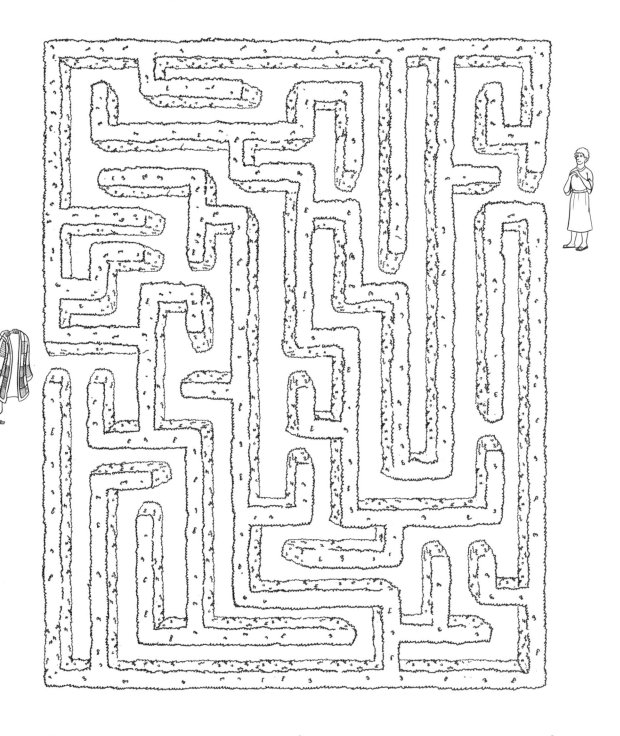

Coat Of Many Colours

Joseph's brothers were very envious of his cool coat! Use your brightest pens and pencils to make it a multicoloured coat to be proud of.

The Story Of Joseph

Can you find these words from the story of Joseph hidden in this wordsearch? The words read forwards, backwards, up, down and diagonally.

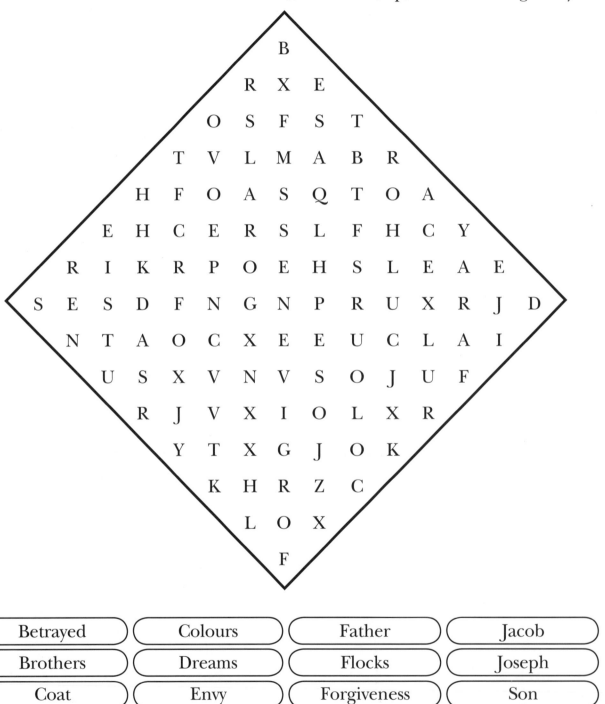

```
                        B
                     R  X  E
                  O  S  F  S  T
               T  V  L  M  A  B  R
            H  F  O  A  S  Q  T  O  A
         E  H  C  E  R  S  L  F  H  C  Y
      R  I  K  R  P  O  E  H  S  L  E  A  E
   S  E  S  D  F  N  G  N  P  R  U  X  R  J  D
      N  T  A  O  C  X  E  E  U  C  L  A  I
         U  S  X  V  N  V  S  O  J  U  F
            R  J  V  X  I  O  L  X  R
               Y  T  X  G  J  O  K
                  K  H  R  Z  C
                     L  O  X
                        F
```

Betrayed	Colours	Father	Jacob
Brothers	Dreams	Flocks	Joseph
Coat	Envy	Forgiveness	Son

Envious Brothers

Joseph's brothers knew he was their dad's favourite and they weren't happy about it at all! Which piece completes this picture of Jacob's sons?

Poor Joseph

Joseph's brothers were so keen to get rid of him that they sold him as a slave. Use your pencils or pens to colour the picture using the key below.

1 Red **2** Green **3** Brown
4 Blue **5** Yellow **6** Orange

Off To Egypt

Which of these brothers did a deal with a trader and agreed a price for Joseph?

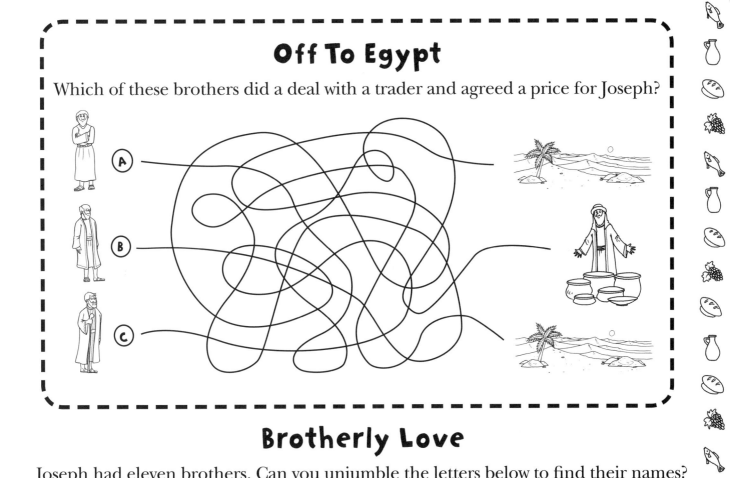

Brotherly Love

Joseph had eleven brothers. Can you unjumble the letters below to find their names?

1. eburne   _ _ _ b _ _
2. eisonm   _ _ _ e _ _
3. lvie   L _ _ _
4. uahdj   _ _ d _ _
5. sicsrhaa   _ _ s _ _ _ _ _
6. uzeubln   _ e _ _ _ _ _
7. jnnmiabe   _ _ _ _ _ m_ _
8. dna   D _ _
9. alahinpt   _ _ _ h _ _ _ _
10. adg   _ _ d
11. share   _ s _ _ _

Hard Work

Whilst imprisoned as a slave, Joseph discovered he could interpret people's dreams. Which piece completes the picture?

The Pharaoh's Dream

The Pharaoh of Egypt often had very strange dreams so he called on Joseph to help interpret them. Colour in this picture of his puzzling dream about cows!

River Bed

A new pharaoh made the Israelites into slaves and threatened to get rid of all Israelite baby boys. Moses' mother hid him in some reeds to keep him safe. Can you spot eight differences between these two pictures?

Furious Pharaoh

The bad-tempered Pharaoh was cross that there were so many Israelites in Egypt. How many new words can you make from the letters in 'Israelites'? The first one is done for you!

ISRAELITES

Star

Moses Baskets

All these pictures of baby Moses in his basket look the same, but one is slightly different from the others. Can you spot which one it is?

Moses Is Saved

The Pharaoh's daughter rescued Moses and promised to take care of him.
Use your pens or pencils to colour in the picture.

Finding Moses

Can you find these words from the story of baby Moses hidden in this wordsearch? The words read forwards, backwards, up, down and diagonally.

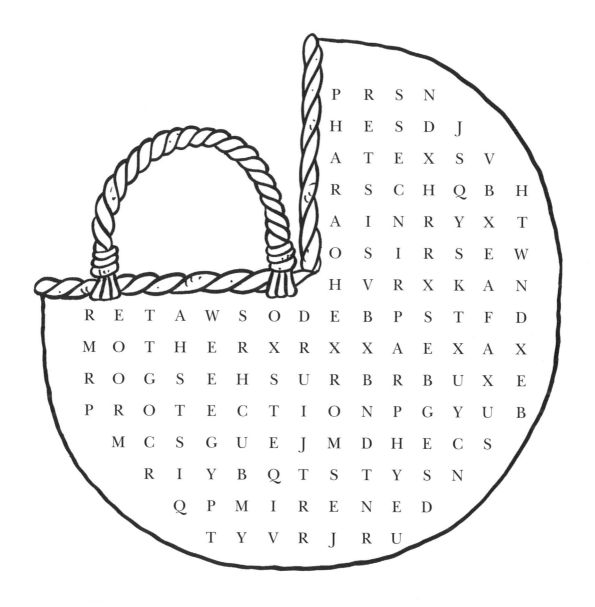

```
              P  R  S  N
              H  E  S  D  J
              A  T  E  X  S  V
              R  S  C  H  Q  B  H
              A  I  N  R  Y  X  T
              O  S  I  R  S  E  W
              H  V  R  X  K  A  N
    R  E  T  A  W  S  O  D  E  B  P  S  T  F  D
    M  O  T  H  E  R  X  R  X  X  A  E  X  A  X
    R  O  G  S  E  H  S  U  R  B  R  B  U  X  E
    P  R  O  T  E  C  T  I  O  N  P  G  Y  U  B
    M  C  S  G  U  E  J  M  D  H  E  C  S
       R  I  Y  B  Q  T  S  T  Y  S  N
       Q  P  M  I  R  E  N  E  D
          T  Y  V  R  J  R  U
```

| Baby | Basket | Daughter | Egypt | Moses |

| Mother | Pharaoh | Princess | Protection | Rescue |

| River | Rushes | Sister | Water |

45

The Second Plague

God sent ten plagues to teach the bad Pharaoh a lesson! Can you find which piece completes this picture of the second plague of frogs.

Spot the Frogs

Egypt was crawling with frogs during the second plague! Look carefully at this picture for 20 seconds and then turn the page to answer the questions.

Plague Picture

Now you've studied the picture on page 47, see if you can answer these questions.

1. How many people are there in the picture?
2. Where is the pile of stones?
3. How many frogs are there in the tree?
4. What is the man in the foreground carrying?
5. What symbol is above the doorway?
6. Apart from frogs, which other two animals are in the picture?
7. How many trees are in the picture?

Bonus question: Which plague came after the frogs?
a) Locusts. b) Insects. c) Ladybirds.

Jumping Frogs

Which way did the frogs hop to reach Egypt?

The Passover

The Israelites painted their houses so that God would know where they were to keep them safe. How many paintbrushes can you spot in the picture?

Freedom Food

A special dinner was held before the Israelites escaped from Egypt. Can you spot the eight differences between these pictures of the Passover meal?

Remember Moses

Once the Israelites were freed from slavery Moses led them towards a new land. Look carefully at this picture for 20 seconds and then turn the page to answer the questions without peeking! You can colour in the picture too!

Moses Memory Game

Once you've studied the picture of Moses leading his people to safety, answer these questions about it.

1. How many women are there in the picture?
2. What is the man directly behind Moses carrying?
3. How many pyramids can you see?
4. What is Moses holding in his left hand?
5. How many birds are sitting in the tree?
6. How many animals can you see in the picture?
7. Is the front door of the first house open or closed?

Bonus question: What happened when the Israelites reached the Red Sea?
a) They went for a paddle. b) They had to swim. c) Moses parted the waves.

A Friend In The Flames

Before Moses took his people out of Egypt, God called out from a burning bush to offer his help. Which way did Moses go to hear God's words?

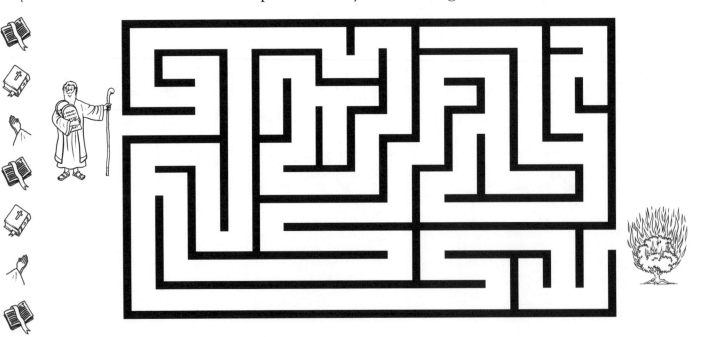

The Red Sea

As Moses and his people got closer to the Red Sea, the Pharaoh's army was hot on their heels! Use your pens or pencils to colour the picture.

Finding Freedom

Can you find these words from the story of Moses hidden in this wordsearch?
The words read forwards, backwards, up, down and diagonally.

```
A  G  T  S  T  O  N  E  T  A  B  L  E  T  E
C  Y  G  Q  Z  K  V  G  D  H  M  D  Q  Z  C
F  P  S  K  Q  P  S  B  L  H  P  A  M  B  R
O  Z  M  C  S  Y  P  T  Q  H  P  J  S  A  E
V  X  O  I  Y  E  N  R  U  O  J  A  E  G  D
K  T  U  F  W  V  P  A  K  R  V  X  C  S
J  F  N  S  D  H  N  A  D  M  G  Y  V  E  E
D  R  T  S  B  Y  Q  G  L  N  M  Q  K  C  A
U  E  S  N  P  N  H  H  Z  S  A  E  S  Z  V
H  E  I  A  G  M  O  S  E  S  E  N  G  B  N
H  D  N  K  K  D  E  F  S  L  S  Y  T  F  Y
B  O  A  E  V  E  F  E  R  Z  C  F  T  K  F
Q  M  I  J  M  R  V  G  U  P  A  L  P  N  Z
S  E  U  G  A  L  P  P  R  P  P  C  I  P  J
A  V  Q  A  Y  K  T  R  E  S  E  D  F  B  W
```

Desert	Journey	Plagues	Snake
Escape	Moses	Red Sea	Stone Tablet
Freedom	Mount Sinai	Slaves	Stick

54

Through The Waves

God helped Moses by parting the Red Sea to make a path through it.
Use your pencils or pens to colour the picture using the key below.

(1) Red (2) Green (3) Brown (4) Blue
(5) Yellow (6) Orange (7) Pink

Moses Maze

Which way did Moses travel to lead his people out of Egypt?

Manna From Heaven

The Israelites had to walk for days through the wilderness, but God sent food when they were hungry. Which piece completes this picture of people collecting the sweet-tasting manna?

A   B   C   D

Missing Moses

Can you fill in the blanks to complete these facts about the story of Moses?

1. Moses asked the P _ _ _ _ _ _ to free his people.

2. When he said no God sent t _ _ plagues to punish the Pharaoh.

3. The I _ _ _ _ _ _ _ _ _ followed Moses out of Egypt.

4. The Pharaoh sent his a _ _ _ to stop Moses and his people leaving.

5. Moses parted the R _ _ S _ _ to help his people escape.

6. God provided a sweet tasting food called m _ _ _ _ to feed the hungry Israelites.

7. God made water flow from M _ _ _ _ S _ _ _ _ to ensure the Israelites had something to drink.

Holy Food

These baskets of manna all look the same, but can you spot which one is different from the others?

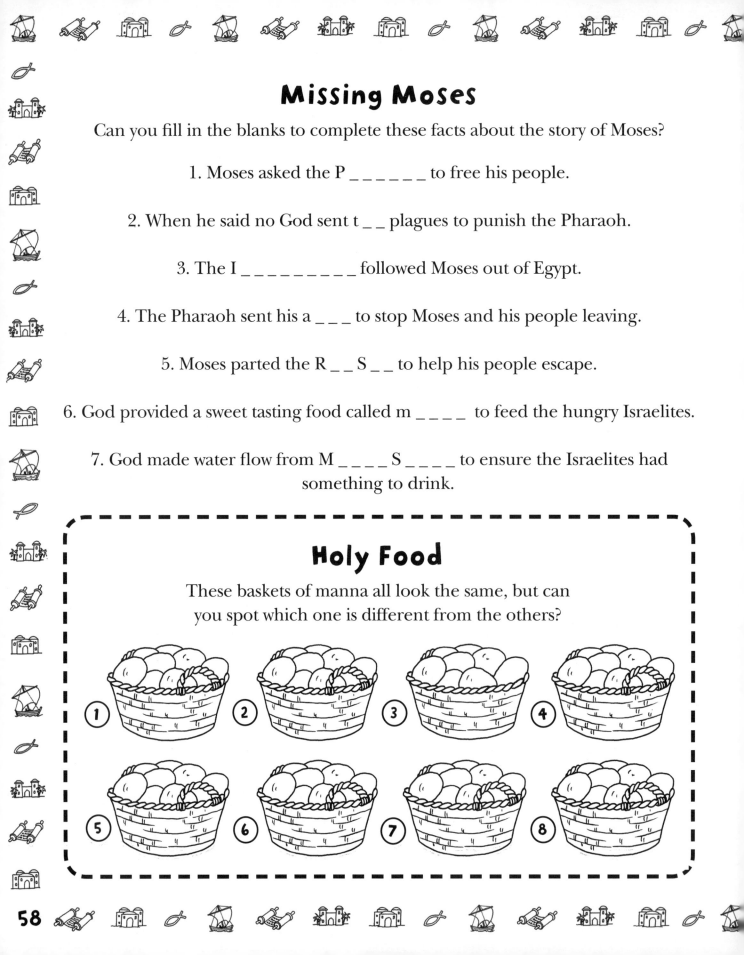

Written In Stone

God gave Moses a list of ten laws, written on two stone tablets. Colour in this picture of Moses looking at the Ten Commandments on Mount Sinai.

Messenger Moses

Moses came back to tell his people about the laws they would follow. How many small stone tablets can you find hidden in the picture? Once you've found them all, colour it in.

Special Stones

Moses was very special, as he was the only one allowed up the mountain to hear God's word. Look carefully at this picture for 20 seconds and then turn the page to answer the questions. You can colour the picture in too!

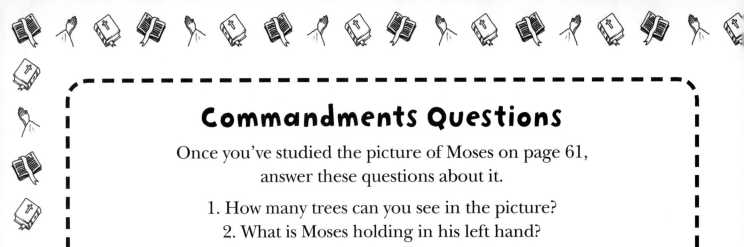

Commandments Questions

Once you've studied the picture of Moses on page 61,
answer these questions about it.

1. How many trees can you see in the picture?
2. What is Moses holding in his left hand?
3. How many clouds are there in the sky?
4. What is Moses wearing on his feet?
5. How many birds are sitting on the rocks?
6. What is the Roman numeral for six?
7. How many birds are flying in the sky?

Bonus question: What is the name of the mountain Moses is standing on?
a) Everest.   b) Sinai.   c) Kilimanjaro.

Mountain Path

Which of these mountain paths did Moses follow
to reach God and the Ten Commandments?

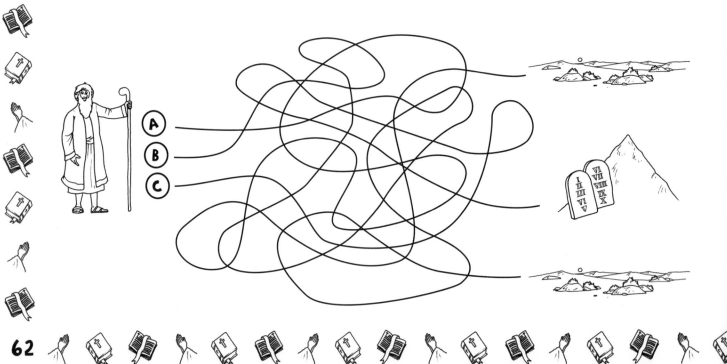

Mountain Mischief

While Moses was gone, his people misbehaved! They melted all their gold together to make a false god. Colour in this picture of the people worshipping a golden calf.

The Laws Of The Land

Can you fill in the blanks to complete the Ten Commandments given to Moses?

1. Thou shall have no other g _ _ _.
2. Thou shall not worship false i _ _ _ _.
3. Thou shall h _ _ _ _ _ God's name.
4. Thou shall honour the S _ _ _ _ _ _ day.
5. Honour your f _ _ _ _ _ and m _ _ _ _ _ .
6. Thou shall not m _ _ _ _ _.
7. Thou shall not commit a _ _ _ _ _ _ _ .
8. Thou shall not s _ _ _ _.
9. Thou shall not b _ _ _ false w _ _ _ _ _ _.
10. Thou shall not c _ _ _ _.

The Golden Calf

These pictures of the golden calf all look the same, but one is different from the rest. Can you spot which is the odd one out?

Moab Bound

The King of Moab panicked when he saw the Israelites approaching his country. He summoned the prophet Balaam to come and curse them! Which piece completes this picture of Balaam beginning his journey?

A   B   C   D

Angel Crossing

God blocked Balaam's path with an angel, but only the donkey could see it. Fill in the missing letters to complete the sentence about the picture.

Balaam's d _ _ _ _ _ stopped when an a _ _ _ _ appeared in front of it.

A Talking Donkey

God made the donkey speak so that Balaam would listen!
Which one of these donkeys is different from the others?

Tumbling Walls

God chose Joshua to lead an army of Israelites into Jericho. Which of his soldiers blew the horn that caused the wall to fall?

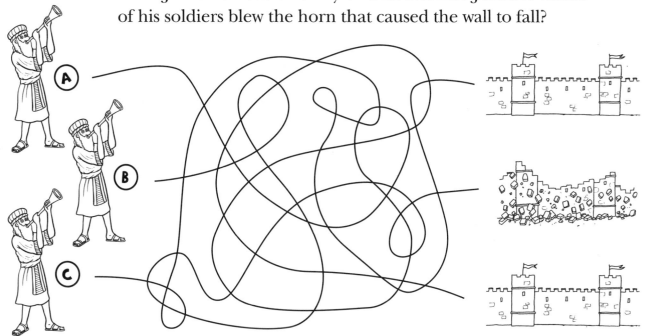

Missing Joshua

Can you fill in these blanks to complete the facts about the story of Joshua?

1. God chose J _ _ _ _ _ to lead an army to J _ _ _ _ _ _.

2. Joshua had his army m _ _ _ _ around the city for s _ _ days.

3. The army marched around the c _ _ _ once every d _ _ _.

4. On the s _ _ _ _ _ _ day they marched around the city s _ _ _ _ times.

5. As they marched they s _ _ _ _ _ _ _ their h _ _ _ _.

6. As they b _ _ _ their horns everyone s _ _ _ _ _ _ and the walls fell.

The Fall Of Jericho

Joshua's soldiers surrounded Jericho for six days, before they made the city walls collapse on the seventh day. Use your favourite pens or pencils to colour in the picture.

Super Strongman

God made Samson amazingly strong so that he could protect the Israelites from the Philistines. Look carefully at this picture for 20 seconds and then see if you can answer the questions on the next page from memory.

Samson's Strength

Now you've studied the picture of Samson on page 69, answer
these questions without looking back at it.

1. How many of the soldiers are holding shields?
2. What design is on the soldiers' shields?
3. How many pillars are collapsing around Samson?
4. What is the soldier in the background doing?
5. How many clouds are there in the sky?
6. What shape is the block by Samson's feet?
7. How many boulders are there on the ground?

Bonus question: In the story, what was the name of the
girl Samson fell in love with?
a) Delilah.   b) Rebekah.   c) Esther.

Spot Samson

Samson was strong enough to kill a lion with his bare hands!
Which picture of Samson is different from the others?

Samson's Secret

Delilah discovered that Samson's strength was in his long hair and she betrayed him by cutting it off. Can you spot the eight differences between these two pictures?

Devious Delilah

Which way did Delilah go to persuade Samson to tell her his secret?

Samson Search

Can you find these words from the story of Samson hidden in the wordsearch? The words read forwards, backwards, up, down and diagonally.

```
I  F  E  S  D        R  X  A  S  K
D  X  D  P  Y        G  G  H  C  C
D  E  E  R  F        N  H  T  R  I
B  U  O  N  W        I  F  G  O  R
R  Y  P  D  J        D  T  N  P  T
I  F  H  E  L        D  L  E  E  Y
D  F  I  L  I        E  H  R  S  Y
D  L  L  I  O        W  E  T  N  S
L  E  I  L  N        W  L  S  O  E
E  G  S  A  C        I  P  U  S  C
V  N  T  H  R        B  M  F  M  R
U  A  I  O  I        I  E  K  A  E
E  Z  N  N  A        X  T  H  S  T
R  R  E  E  H        X  Q  Y  H  H
T  R  S  Y  L        G  U  M  U  M
```

Angel	Hair	Philistines	Samson	Temple
Delilah	Honey	Riddle	Secret	Trick
Freed	Lion	Ropes	Strength	Wedding

Special Places

Can you find these biblical places hidden in the wordsearch? The words read forwards, backwards, up, down and diagonally.

```
R  G  Q  P  N  E  E  N  P  O  P  Z  Q  Y  V
W  X  Q  R  Q  U  O  H  C  I  R  E  J  N  H
M  A  E  S  D  A  E  D  L  H  O  S  O  A  R
S  B  N  A  A  N  A  C  T  P  Y  G  E  Z  A
M  E  H  E  L  H  T  E  B  E  J  D  F  A  Q
O  W  H  B  L  Y  Q  U  E  M  Z  B  F  R  Z
M  F  G  W  L  M  T  L  E  F  A  E  E  E  V
U  G  N  N  Y  C  I  L  H  B  N  D  E  T  G
S  W  I  O  O  L  A  S  Y  H  S  Q  I  H  D
E  S  N  K  A  S  U  L  L  E  I  X  S  V  Q
L  A  E  G  U  U  O  Y  A  X  D  O  O  K
K  F  V  R  T  N  E  O  Q  L  K  N  U  P  G
Z  Q  E  D  V  W  H  W  P  X  V  F  G  Y  S
H  J  H  C  W  C  A  N  E  V  A  E  H  O  I
Y  O  G  U  F  Y  S  Q  G  E  A  Y  L  E  R
```

Babylon	Dead Sea	Heaven	Nazareth
Bethlehem	Egypt	Jericho	Nineveh
Canaan	Galilee	Jerusalem	Red Sea

Gathering Grain

Ruth was a widow who moved to Bethlehem with Naomi, her mother-in-law. Boaz was a kind relative of Naomi and let Ruth have some of his grain. Look at the picture for 20 seconds and then turn the page to answer the questions.

Remember Ruth

Ruth and Boaz got married and their great grandson David later became King of Israel. Now you've studied their picture on page 75, try answering these questions.

1. How many bundles of grain have been harvested behind Boaz?
2. How many trees are in the picture?
3. How many pears are on the pear trees?
4. How many workers are in the field with Ruth and Boaz?
5. What kind of object is by Ruth's feet?
6. How many windows does the house in the background have?
7. What is Ruth holding in her arms?

Bonus question: Who moved to Bethlehem with Ruth?
a) Her grandmother.   b) Her mother-in-law.   c) Her friend.

Fields Of Gold

Which of these paths leads to the field where there is still grain to be harvested?

Kind Boaz

Boaz promised to look after Naomi and Ruth while they were in Bethlehem. Which piece completes this picture?

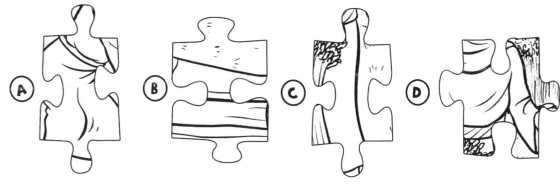

Hannah's Prayer

Hannah didn't have any children so she prayed to God for a
son. How many flowers can you find hidden in this picture?
Once you've found them all, colour in the picture.

Special Son

Hannah had promised to give her son back to God so she took Samuel to work with Eli the priest. Can you spot the eight differences between these two pictures?

People Of The Bible

Can you find these people from the bible hidden in the wordsearch?
The names read forwards, backwards, up, down and diagonally.

```
M  S  W  F  B  V  D  L  D  B  E  L  X  Z  Q
V  M  A  P  D  Z  Q  T  D  O  V  Z  I  G  V
V  P  F  M  U  T  A  Y  R  A  Z  Y  N  S  I
E  A  U  H  S  O  J  H  Z  Z  V  O  G  K  E
W  A  E  N  A  O  M  D  T  D  A  I  V  A  H
Y  A  X  H  S  U  N  X  N  H  C  F  D  O  T
Y  Z  B  U  Z  D  T  Y  Z  G  G  K  B  H  N
E  A  B  R  A  H  A  M  D  A  M  M  A  D  A
B  O  Z  D  I  M  S  V  V  Q  N  H  K  X  O
E  V  E  R  E  B  E  K  A  H  I  A  Y  E  M
F  F  M  R  G  L  A  F  S  R  R  N  Q  L  I
Y  B  J  P  B  Z  I  A  R  U  J  N  W  L  X
N  S  T  G  U  T  R  L  A  T  Y  A  J  B  Y
C  T  W  I  R  A  B  M  A  H  A  H  B  A  O
J  Y  K  S  H  I  Z  A  X  H  F  L  D  E  R
```

Abraham	David	Hannah	Noah
Adam	Delilah	Joshua	Rebekah
Boaz	Eve	Naomi	Ruth
	Samson	Sarah	

A New King

Samuel became a prophet, and God told him that Israel was to have a new king, the youngest son of Jesse. Fill in the missing letters to complete the sentence.

The shepherd boy D _ _ _ _ was chosen to become the future King of I _ _ _ _ _.

Harp Harmony

Young David was a very good harpist. Which of these harps is different from the others?

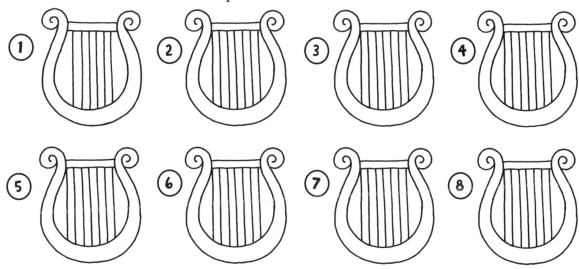

Young Musician

David had a talent for singing, too. His songs, or psalms, are still sung today. Colour the picture using the number guide below.

① Grey ② Light Green ③ Brown ④ Blue
⑤ Yellow ⑥ Dark Green ⑦ Pink

David vs Goliath

David was much smaller than the mighty Goliath, but he had the strength of God to help him. Which way did David go to defeat Goliath?

Sling Search

Can you find these words from the story of David and Goliath hidden in this wordsearch? The words read forwards, backwards, up, down and diagonally.

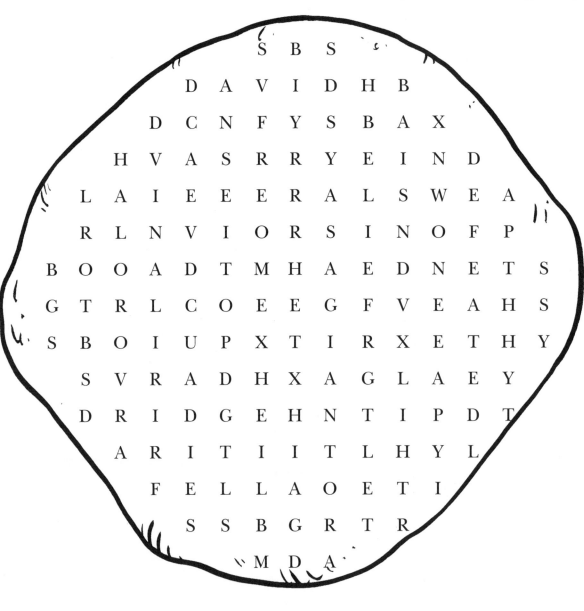

```
              S  B  S
           D  A  V  I  D  H  B
        D  C  N  F  Y  S  B  A  X
     H  V  A  S  R  R  Y  E  I  N  D
     L  A  I  E  E  R  A  L  S  W  E  A
     R  L  N  V  I  O  R  S  I  N  O  F  P
  B  O  O  A  D  T  M  H  A  E  D  N  E  T  S
  G  T  R  L  C  O  E  E  G  F  V  E  A  H  S
  S  B  O  I  U  P  X  T  I  R  X  E  T  H  Y
     S  V  R  A  D  H  X  A  G  L  A  E  Y
     D  R  I  D  G  E  H  N  T  I  P  D  T
     A  R  I  T  I  I  T  L  H  Y  L
     F  E  L  L  A  O  E  T  I
        S  S  B  G  R  T  R
              M  D  A
```

Afraid	Belief	Defeated	Goliath	Soldiers
Armour	Bravery	Fight	Shepherd	Stones
Battle	David	Giant	Sling	Victory

Brave David

David faced Goliath with only his sling and a few stones! Look carefully at this picture for 20 seconds and then see if you can answer the questions on the next page from memory.

Question Time

Now you've studied the picture of David and Goliath on page 85, try to answer these questions without peeking back at it.

1. How many leaves are there on the tree?
2. What is the symbol on Goliath's shield?
3. How many soldiers are on horseback?
4. What is David holding?
5. How many sheep are there in the field?
6. What is David throwing at Goliath?
7. How many boulders are there in the picture?

Bonus question: What did young David work as?
a) A cheese maker.   b) A shepherd boy.   c) A cook.

Home Sweet Home

Can you remember where these people lived? See if you can match them all to the places they called home.

1. Adam and Eve	A. Bethlehem
2. Abraham	B. Egypt
3. Moses	C. Garden of Eden
4. Samson	D. Israel
5. Naomi, Ruth and Boaz	E. Canaan

Champion Israelite

With God on his side, David was able to defeat the 10 foot tall giant Goliath and the Philistine's fled. Can you spot the eight differences between these two pictures?

A Royal Visit

When David died, his son Solomon became King of Israel. The Queen of Sheba came to visit the new king in Jerusalem. How many new words can you make from the letters in 'Jerusalem'? The first one is done for you!

JERUSALEM

.... Mules ....

....

....

....

Kind Queen

The Queen's many camels were laden with gifts for King Solomon. Which of these camels is different from the others?

Royal Riches

The visiting queen came from a very rich country. Use silver, gold and other brightly coloured pens to colour in this picture of the Queen of Sheba.

Guidance From God

King Solomon prayed in his temple for God to help him become a great leader. How many crowns can you find hidden in the picture? Once you've found them all, colour it in.

The First Temple

Solomon spent many years building a wonderful temple for God.
Which piece completes the picture of God's first temple?

Healing Naaman

Naaman was an important army general, but he had a terrible disease. A wise prophet told him to bathe in the River Jordan to heal himself. Can you show Naaman the way to the river?

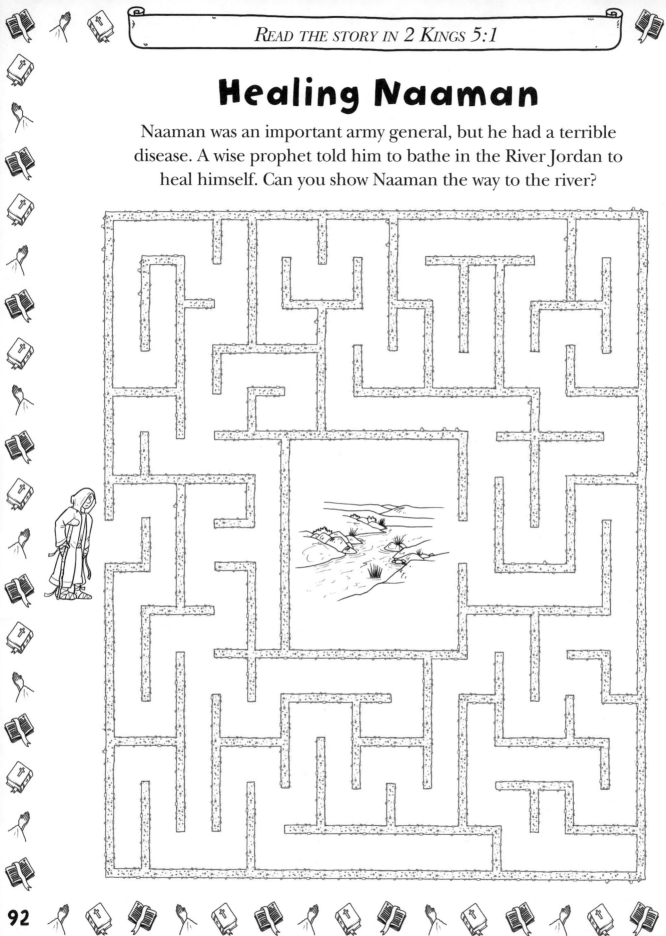

River Miracle

The prophet told Naaman to wash himself in the river Jordan seven times, and it worked – he was cured! Which jigsaw piece do you need to complete the scene?

A

B

C

D

Jonah's Lesson

Jonah tried to go somewhere else when God asked him to go to Nineveh, so God sent a hurricane in anger. How many new words can you make from the letters in 'hurricane'? The first one is done for you!

HURRICANE

Rain ....

....

....

....

Find The Fishing Boat

The boat that Jonah sailed on is slightly different to all the other ones on the sea. Can you spot which one it is?

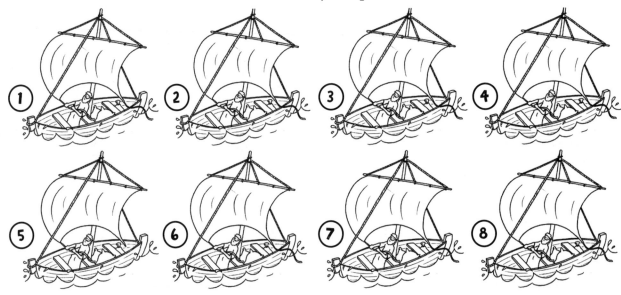

Jonah And The Whale

The prophet Jonah was thrown into the sea during a fierce storm and swallowed by a giant whale! Study this underwater scene for 20 seconds and then turn the page to answer the questions.

Jonah's Memory Game

Now you've studied the picture of Jonah and the whale on page 95,
try answering these questions without looking back. No cheating!

1. How many fish can you see on the whale's tail?
2. Which animal is sitting on the shipwreck?
3. How many crabs are there in the picture?
4. What pattern does the fish in the seaweed have on its body?
5. How many teeth can you see in the whale's mouth?
6. Is the clamshell open or closed?
7. How many limpets are stuck to the rock in the foreground?

Bonus question: Which city did God tell Jonah to visit
before he was shipwrecked?
a) Joppa.   b) Nineveh.   c) Jerusalem.

Whale Tangle

God sent a whale to save Jonah from drowning. Follow the
tangled lines to find out which one leads to the whale.

There She Blows!

After three days, God told the mighty whale to release Jonah from his giant belly.
Can you find eight differences between these two pictures of Jonah's narrow escape?

Whale Wordsearch

Can you find these words from the story of Jonah hidden in this wordsearch?
The words read forwards, backwards, up, down and diagonally.

```
H  J  Y  X  S  M  P  R  A  Y  I  N  G  S  D
S  E  V  A  W  A  T  M  R  U  Q  X  S  Q  Z
S  G  E  S  W  A  L  L  O  W  E  D  U  P  J
V  F  K  O  V  B  S  B  O  A  T  N  F  J  E
S  A  V  E  D  N  E  V  I  M  S  Z  C  A  Q
Y  M  I  D  J  D  U  R  P  J  R  G  D  R  S
E  L  S  O  I  T  E  N  C  Q  E  O  B  R  A
F  M  N  E  Y  U  V  T  K  T  P  V  X  I  I
F  A  N  V  I  L  A  W  X  M  E  E  N  A  L
H  C  D  C  Q  Z  L  F  K  G  N  R  M  S  O
E  O  C  E  A  N  M  E  S  F  T  B  C  E  R
Q  D  R  K  X  R  L  E  B  L  C  O  N  A  S
B  T  G  C  O  A  N  D  B  D  U  A  P  E  G
N  Y  I  T  H  W  X  H  T  W  M  R  V  L  Z
A  N  S  W  Y  M  V  A  B  Z  C  D  F  C  N
```

Boat	Obedience	Praying	Saved	Swallowed
Belly	Ocean	Repent	Sea	Waves
Jonah	Overboard	Sailors	Storm	Whale

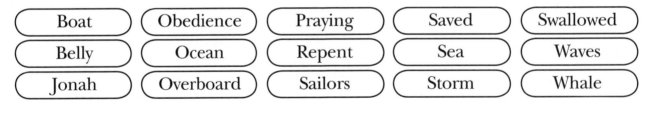

The King's Mistake

King Belshazzar thought he had as much power as God because he had so many riches. Use your favourite pens or pencils to colour in this picture of the king in his palace.

Writing On The Wall

King Belshazzar arranged a great banquet during which his guests worshipped many other gods. During the feast, a floating hand appeared and began to write on the wall. Which jigsaw piece do you need to complete this incredible scene?

Belshazzar's Search

Can you find these words from the story of Belshazzar hidden in this wordsearch? The words read forwards, backwards, up, down and diagonally.

```
E  N  O  B  L  E  S  H  V  T  V  L  U  F  D
N  R  Z  Y  R  C  A  I  E  S  H  L  Y  A  J
S  V  B  R  E  G  L  H  L  E  M  A  H  Z  W
H  L  A  D  Q  G  N  E  V  V  K  W  X  N  Y
E  P  N  W  T  V  W  I  T  F  E  K  U  K  J
G  A  Q  I  S  E  L  W  N  Z  D  R  F  S  G
H  V  U  X  J  T  S  M  A  R  X  H  H  T  Y
Q  L  E  G  N  I  K  S  F  T  A  K  L  S  E
W  N  T  D  Q  O  C  Z  D  D  Z  W  W  D  J
I  U  O  F  W  R  I  T  I  N  G  K  J  T  Z
V  P  D  L  B  E  L  S  H  A  Z  Z  A  R  F
O  P  Y  J  Y  K  B  O  R  G  Q  Y  F  T  P
I  G  P  M  V  B  K  K  B  I  O  T  G  Y  I
R  J  T  R  Y  D  A  U  I  F  W  K  R  U  K
Y  R  M  S  E  T  V  B  W  C  G  G  O  L  D
```

Babylon	Gold	King	Wall
Banquet	Hand	Nobles	Warning
Belshazzar	Jewels	Silver	Writing

Daniel And The Lions

Daniel was thrown into a dark lions' den for praying to God. How many candles can you find in this picture? Once you've found them all, colour it in.

Daniel's Prayer

Daniel's faith saved him from the lions. Can you lead him
through the maze and show him the way out of the den?

Lion Look-a-likes

The lions didn't hurt Daniel, as God was protecting him. Can you spot which of the lions is different from the others?

Angel Tangle

God sent an angel to keep the lions away. Untangle the lines to find out which angel looked after Daniel.

Daniel's Wordsearch

Can you find these words from the story of Daniel hidden in the wordsearch?
The words read forwards, backwards, up, down and diagonally.

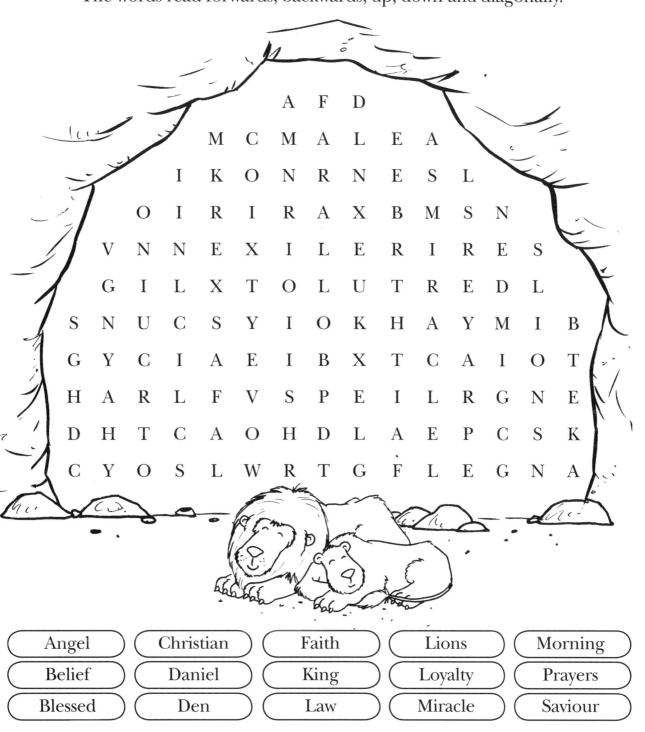

```
        A F D
      M C M A L E A
        I K O N R N E S L
      O I R I R A X B M S N
    V N N E X I L E R I R E S
    G I L X T O L U T R E D L
  S N U C S Y I O K H A Y M I B
  G Y C I A E I B X T C A I O T
  H A R L F V S P E I L R G N E
  D H T C A O H D L A E P C S K
  C Y O S L W R T G F L E G N A
```

Angel	Christian	Faith	Lions	Morning
Belief	Daniel	King	Loyalty	Prayers
Blessed	Den	Law	Miracle	Saviour

Guardian Angel

Colour the picture of Daniel and the angel using the number guide below.

① Red ② Green ③ Brown
④ Blue ⑤ Yellow ⑥ Orange

Nehemiah's Request

When Nehemiah heard that Jerusalem was in ruins, he wanted to go there and offer his help. Use your favourite pens or pencils to colour this picture of Nehemiah asking the king if he can return to the city.

City Saviour

Nehemiah remembered how beautiful Jerusalem used to be and was determined to make the city great again. How many new words can you make from the letters in his name? The first one is done for you!

NEHEMIAH

Mine

....

....

....

....

Journey To Jerusalem

Which way did Nehemiah go to help rebuild the city of Jerusalem?

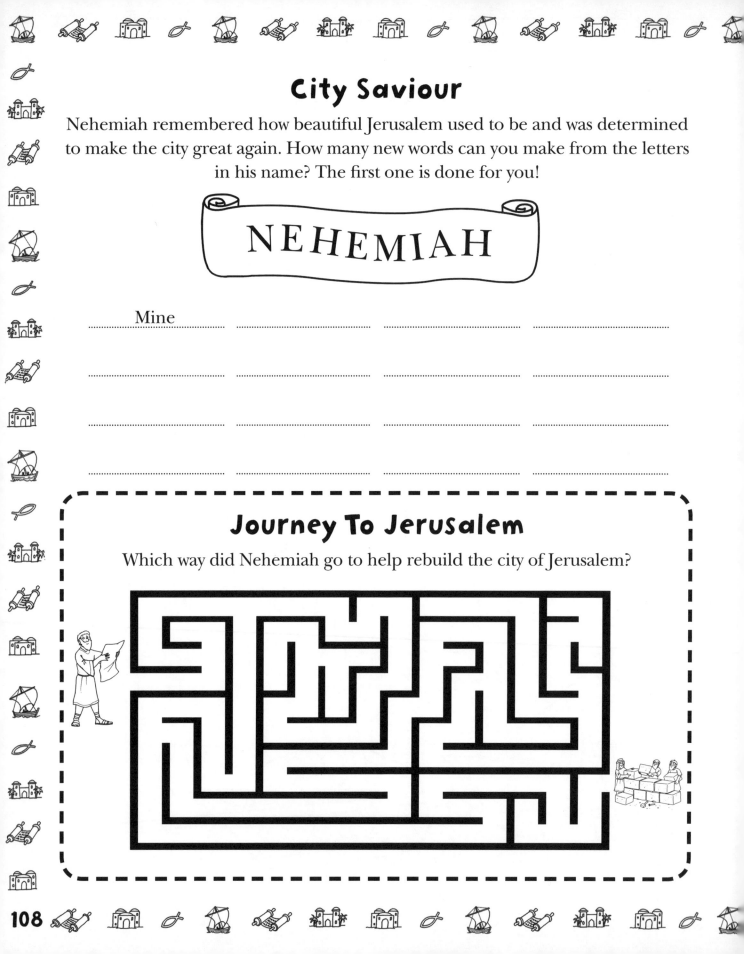

Psalms Search

Can you find these books of the Old Testament hidden in this wordsearch?
The words read forwards, backwards, up, down and diagonally.

```
X  I  G  L  U  X  R  P  S  O  E  J  Z  M  B
W  J  W  P  G  E  B  G  M  C  C  O  S  Q  E
D  T  O  A  T  B  G  E  L  A  C  S  U  B  H
N  U  M  B  F  M  V  N  A  R  L  H  C  B  G
G  O  G  B  W  A  A  E  S  Z  E  U  I  V  E
S  M  K  Y  A  L  B  S  P  E  S  A  T  P  E
R  X  Y  W  D  A  B  I  T  A  I  W  I  D  U
W  D  I  M  A  C  P  S  J  M  A  L  V  K  S
B  A  H  O  N  H  B  X  Y  I  S  O  E  E  R
S  A  O  V  I  I  S  L  L  K  T  E  L  U  E
S  I  M  C  E  Y  S  U  H  L  E  R  V  F  B
K  C  U  W  L  U  M  T  D  V  S  N  S  P  M
B  C  S  E  G  D  U  J  J  O  G  F  P  M  U
T  Q  H  K  H  R  F  P  X  H  X  G  A  C  N
H  H  A  I  A  S  I  T  K  Y  G  E  F  Z  W
```

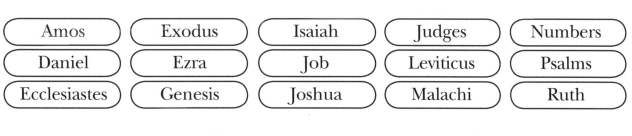

Amos	Exodus	Isaiah	Judges	Numbers
Daniel	Ezra	Job	Leviticus	Psalms
Ecclesiastes	Genesis	Joshua	Malachi	Ruth

Angel Gabriel

The Angel Gabriel was God's most special messenger!
Use your favourite pens or pencils to colour him in.

Mary's Message

God sent Gabriel to speak to a woman in Nazareth whose name was Mary.
Look carefully at this picture for 20 seconds and then turn the page to
answer the questions from memory.

Mary's Memory Game

Now you've studied the picture on the previous page, see if you can answer these questions without peeking back.

1. How many cups are hanging on the wall?
2. What is the pattern on the cups?
3. How many candle lights are there in the picture?
4. What is in the bowl on the table?
5. What is propped in the corner of the room?
6. What is in the vase on the table?
7. What is hanging from a hook below the bottom shelf?

Bonus question: What did the angel tell Mary?
a) That a flood was coming.   b) That she should go to Nineveh.
c) That she would have a baby son called Jesus.

Angel Assembly

Gabriel was one of God's many angels. Which one of these winged messengers is different from the others?

① ② ③ ④
⑤ ⑥ ⑦ ⑧

Joseph the Carpenter

Joseph was Mary's husband-to-be, so an angel brought him a message too!
Which piece completes this picture of Joseph at work?

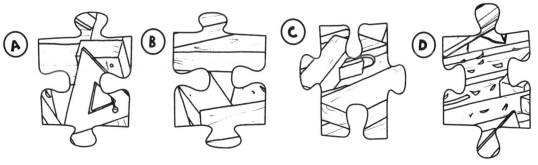

Happy Couple

Mary and Joseph were very excited about their special baby.
Can you spot the eight differences between these pictures of them?

Guardian Angels

Mary and Joseph had to travel from Nazareth to Bethlehem. It was a very long walk but they knew the angels would look after them. How many angels can you find hidden in the picture? Once you've found them all, colour it in!

Busy Bethlehem

Mary and Joseph searched all over Bethlehem for a place to stay but every inn was full. Finally they were offered a warm stable for the night. Can you help them find their way there?

A Child Is Born

Mary's baby was born while she and Joseph were staying in the stable. Fill in the missing letters to describe the picture.

In this story, the baby J _ _ _ _ slept in a m _ _ _ _ _ _ .

A Place To Stay

A bright star shone over the stable on the night Jesus was born. All these stables look the same but the one that is different is where Jesus was born. Can you spot which stable is different?

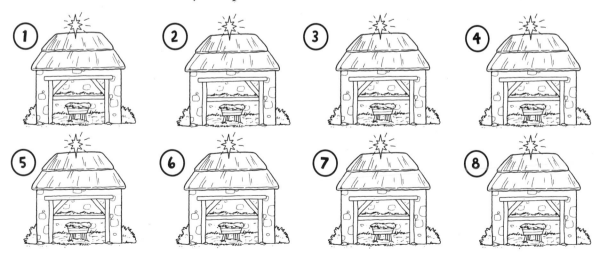

A Special Day

The day that Jesus was born would be remembered for thousands of years to come. Follow the number guide to colour in this bright nativity scene.

(1) Grey (2) Green (3) Light Brown (4) Blue
(5) Yellow (6) Dark brown (7) Orange

Night Light

An angel told a group of shepherds that Jesus had been born. The dazzling light had startled the shepherds, but the angel told them not to be afraid. Can you spot the eight differences between these two pictures?

While Shepherds Watched

After hearing the good news the shepherds set off to visit baby Jesus. One of these shepherds left his crook behind. Can you work out which one?

Nativity Names

Look carefully at these word jumbles. Can you put each set of letters in the right order to spell out words belonging to the nativity story?

1. sjpeoh   ....

2. keonyd   ....

3. sujes   ....

4. hesheedrsp   ....

5. yamr   ....

6. lebhtemeh   ....

We Three Kings

Wise men in the East heard the good news too and followed the star to find Jesus. Which piece completes this picture?

Nativity Wordsearch

Can you find these words from the Nativity story hidden in this wordsearch?
The words read forwards, backwards, up, down and diagonally.

```
I A W F V X M E H E L H T E B
I W O U D A L Y W I S E M E N
K E T O R D O T R R A T S I N
B A B Y J E S U S R I T S X G
H H I Y L S A M A Z H I M X O
P E G E S N E C N I K N A R F
E L B K O D X K B S W I N L L
S B X N L E       H L E G N A
O A L O E T       M E D E T H
J T G D T O       H S I R H T
A S M R S X       A Y B E I F
```

Angel · Bethlehem · Frankincense · Joseph · Mary
Baby Jesus · Donkey · Gold · Manger · Myrrh
Stable · Star · Wise Men

Star Study

The kings wanted to take precious gifts to the special newborn baby. Look carefully at this picture for 20 seconds and then turn the page to answer the questions from memory.

Memory Game

Now you've studied the picture of the wise men on page 123,
see if you can answer these questions without looking back!

1. How many gold coins are there on the floor?
2. What is the servant in the doorway holding?
3. How many trunks are there in the picture?
4. What can be seen out of the window?
5. How many candles are there on the wall?
6. Which fruit is in the dish on the table?
7. How many of the kings are wearing crowns?

Bonus question: Who asked the wise men to let him know where Jesus was?
a) Herod. b) Zechariah. c) Augustus.

Eastern Treasures

The wise men brought gifts of gold, frankincense and myrrh.
Which set of gifts is different from the others?

Herod's Anger

King Herod was furious to hear that the Messiah had been born.
Which piece completes the picture of him plotting with his advisors?

Fleeing Herod

Mary and Joseph had to leave the stable quickly to keep Jesus safe from Herod. Which line leads them to the donkey that helped them on their journey?

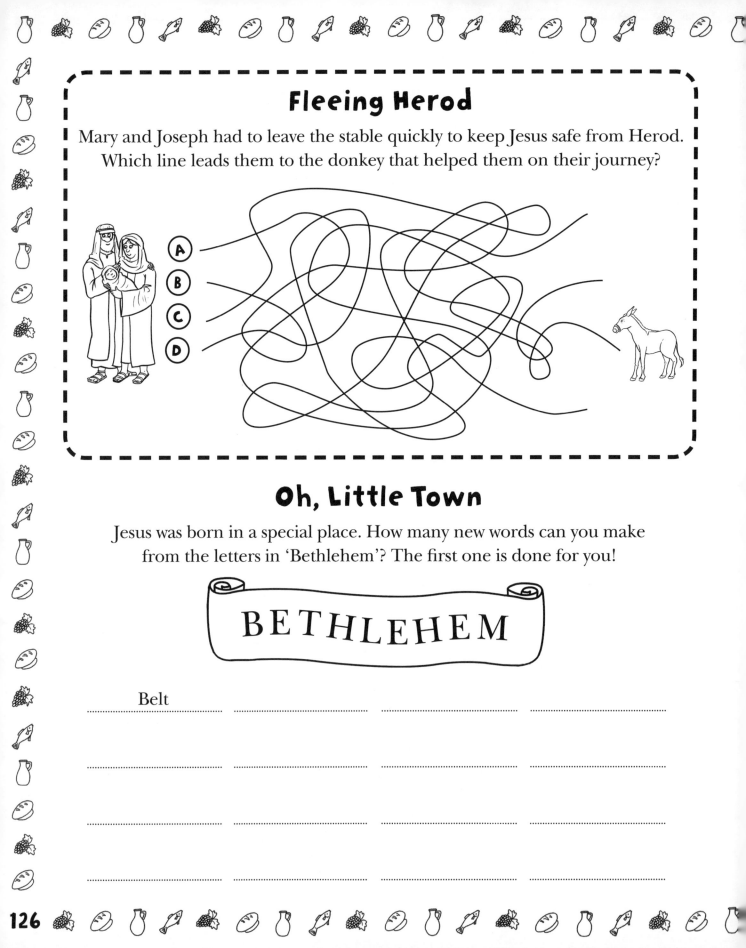

A
B
C
D

Oh, Little Town

Jesus was born in a special place. How many new words can you make from the letters in 'Bethlehem'? The first one is done for you!

BETHLEHEM

Belt

Egypt Bound

An angel told Joseph that his family should escape to Egypt.
Can you spot the eight differences between these two pictures of
Mary, Joseph and Baby Jesus leaving Bethlehem?

READ THE STORY IN MATTHEW 3:13

Jesus Is Baptised

When Jesus was older, John baptised him. How many goblets can you find hidden in this picture of the two cousins? Once you've found them all, colour it in.

Just John

Can you find these words from the story of John the Baptist hidden in this wordsearch? The words read forwards, backwards, up, down and diagonally.

```
D O S N N G M X P O Y X E H D
M E C N A T N E P E R A M F H
U W Z G O K H H V F N J Z B G
R Y C R L O T G L D A T C E P
E Z A C H A R I A H D N R A R
V B E H E A D I N G R A E P O
I A B C O U S I N E O N T W P
R Y T R A M N V M O J X A K H
Y U Y J M Y C O Z J Q R W R E
Z J W D M A L G S I I S G L T
H E R O D A B M S J P T P N V V
E Z L B S R T B H V J P I E V
N O I T A C I F I R U P V O K
X C T W S J R P B R B G I Z F
M S I T P A B A J F Q C L S K
```

Baptism	Herod	Prophet	River Jordan
Beheading	Living Water	Purification	Salome
Cousin	Martyr	Repentance	Zachariah

Friendly Fishermen

While Jesus was strolling by the Sea of Galilee, He noticed some fishermen casting their nets. Use your favourite pens or pencils to colour in this picture.

Follow Me

Jesus asked the fishermen to become his followers and they happily agreed. Which way did the first disciples go to reach Jesus?

Spreading The Word

Jesus said he would teach the fishermen to begin a new life helping others.
Use your pencils or pens to colour the picture using the key below.

① Red ② Green ③ Brown
④ Blue ⑤ Yellow ⑥ Orange

God's Workers

Jesus chose twelve special helpers from his many followers.
Which piece completes this picture of Jesus with his disciples?

Disciple Difference

All these men look the same, but can you spot
which disciple is different from the others?

Finding James

Jesus wanted to speak to his disciple James. Trace the path he took to reach him.

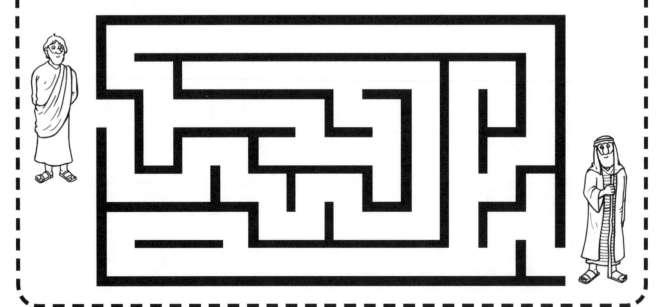

Name Game

Can you find the names of the twelve disciples hidden in this wordsearch?
The words read backwards, forwards, up, down and diagonally.

```
J C O D N O A J G C N K R Q J
H W U Y T W Y A W Z P H X S I
F W E H T T A M X S B S O L L
T Y U T T L K E I A Z A J J U
S O X J B W P S R D P M E E R
R X A H X H C T X U T O P G E
L F B A S A H H F J H H Y X T
J F U G R O E E V O A T M M E
Q H N I L V R Y A N D R E W P
B F O O N S V O U U D K V W N
Z T M B M C Y U E J A M E S O
K E I O G I K N M D E S E L M
W R E T E P S G Y N U M X U I
R H W F G W D E Z F S O X I S
K D R M F D B R O P I L I H P
```

Andrew	James the younger	Matthew	Peter
Bartholomew	John	Philip	Thaddaeus
James	Judas Iscariot	Simon	Thomas

135

Wedding Miracle

Jesus was at a wedding celebration when the wine ran out. He asked the servants to fill six stone jars with water and turned the contents into wine! Use your favourite pens or pencils to colour the picture of this miracle.

A Helping Hand

Jesus' mother Mary was with him when the miracle took place.
Fill in the missing letters to describe what happened.

M _ _ _ persuaded Jesus to perform his f _ _ _ _ miracle
so that there would be enough wine for the guests.

Water Or Wine?

Look carefully at this tangle. Can you find out
which of these jars of water was turned into wine?

The Lord Knows

Jesus impressed the woman by Jacob's well by showing his knowledge of her life even though they had never met before. How many buckets can you find hidden in the picture? Once you've found them all, colour it in!

Feeding The Followers

Jesus had thousands of hungry followers around him and performed a miracle to feed them all. Look carefully at the picture for 20 seconds and then turn the page to answer the questions without looking back at it.

Miracle Memory Game

Now you've studied the picture on page 139 see if you can answer these questions from memory.

1. How many men are on the boat?
2. What is the small boy giving to Jesus?
3. How many baskets of fish are there in the picture?
4. How many women are in the picture?
5. How many baskets of bread are there in the picture?
6. Which shape is on the sail of the boat?
7. How many trees are on the hills in the background?

Bonus question: In the story, Jesus asked the boy to share his food with the crowd. How many items of food did the boy have?
a) One loaf and one fish.   b) Two loaves and two fishes.   c) Five loaves and two fishes.

Packed Lunches

These baskets of food all look the same, but can you spot which one is different from the others?

Loaves And Fishes

Can you find these words from the story of Jesus feeding the five thousand hidden in this wordsearch? The words read forwards, backwards, up, down and diagonally.

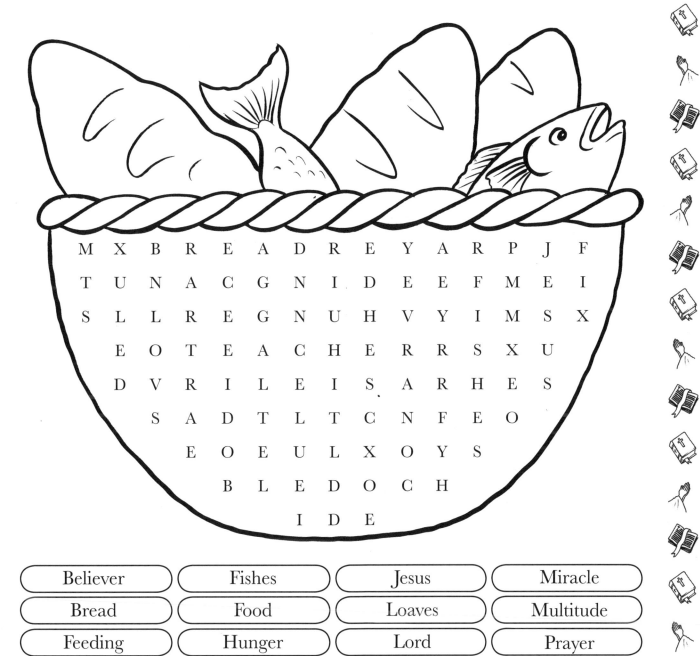

```
M  X  B  R  E  A  D  R  E  Y  A  R  P  J  F
T  U  N  A  C  G  N  I  D  E  E  F  M  E  I
S  L  L  R  E  G  N  U  H  V  Y  I  M  S  X
E  O  T  E  A  C  H  E  R  R  S  X  U
D  V  R  I  L  E  I  S  A  R  H  E  S
   S  A  D  T  L  T  C  N  F  E  O
   E  O  E  U  L  X  O  Y  S
   B  L  E  D  O  C  H
      I  D  E
```

Believer	Fishes	Jesus	Miracle
Bread	Food	Loaves	Multitude
Feeding	Hunger	Lord	Prayer
	Teacher		

Picnic Of Plenty

Jesus created lots of food for the crowd and there was even some left over! Which way did Jesus go to feed his people?

Truly Thankful

The crowds of grateful people were able to eat delicious fish and bread until they felt full. Can you spot the eight differences between these pictures of Jesus feeding the five thousand?

Healing Hands

Jesus became well known for helping sick people. Use your favourite pens or pencils to colour in this picture of Jesus performing a healing miracle.

A Child In Need

Jesus was asked to heal many poorly children. Which way did he walk through the streets to offer help to this boy?

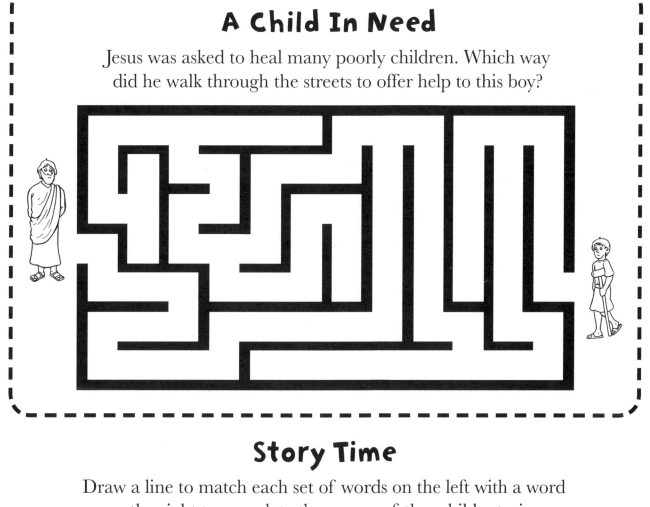

Story Time

Draw a line to match each set of words on the left with a word on the right to complete the names of these bible stories.

1. Samson and	Ten Commandments
2. Moses and the	Baptist
3. Noah's	Goliath
4. The Twelve	Delilah
5. John the	Disciples
6. David and	Ark

Seeing Again

A blind man asked Jesus to take pity on him. Use your pencils or pens
to colour the picture using the key below.

① Red ② Green ③ Brown ④ Blue
⑤ Yellow ⑥ Orange ⑦ Pink

Sudden Storm

The disciples felt afraid when a storm whipped up waves around
their boat on the Sea of Galilee. Which piece completes this picture?

A Good Catch

Some of the disciples were fishermen before Jesus asked them to help with God's work. Which of these fishermen caught a net full of fish?

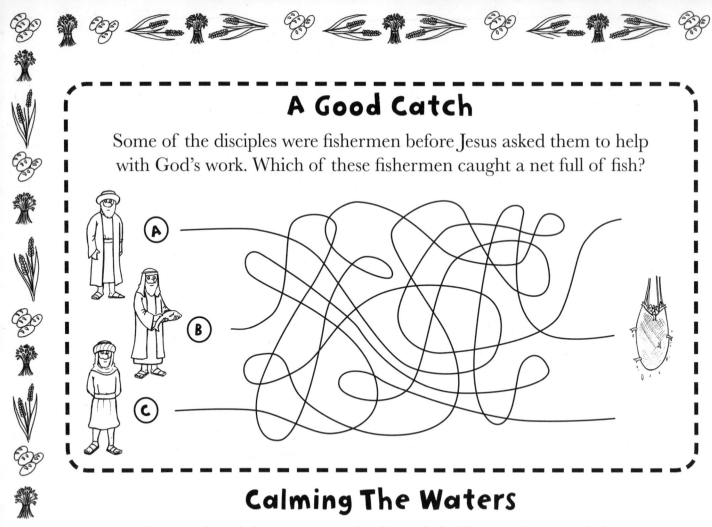

Calming The Waters

Jesus calmed the storm on the Sea of Galilee and stopped the boat from sinking. How many new words can you make from the letters in 'Galilee'? The first one is done for you!

GALILEE

Glee ....

....

....

....

Walking On Water

The disciples were stunned when Jesus walked on water to reach their boat! Use your pens or pencils to colour in this picture of the miracle.

Worship Wordsearch

Jesus was also called 'Christ' or 'The Anointed One' and his teachings formed a religion called Christianity. Can you find these Christian words hidden in the wordsearch? They read forwards, backwards, up, down and diagonally.

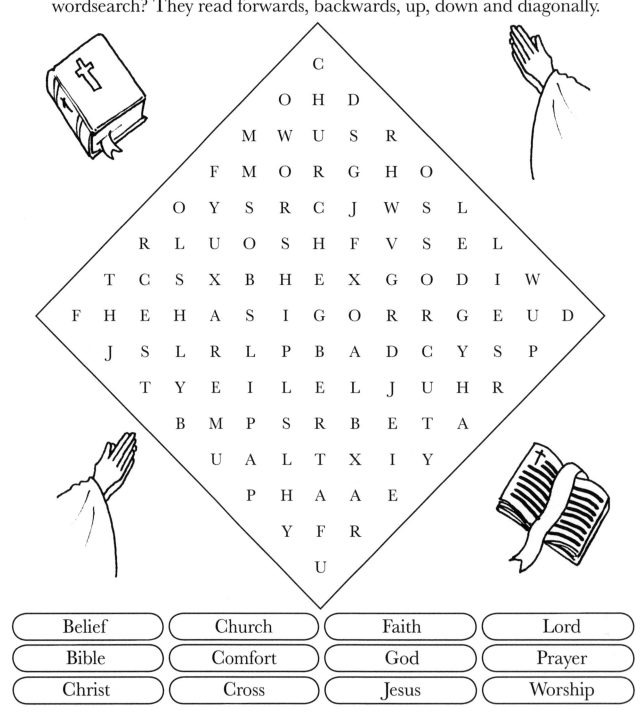

```
                    C
                 O  H  D
              M  W  U  S  R
           F  M  O  R  G  H  O
        O  Y  S  R  C  J  W  S  L
     R  L  U  O  S  H  F  V  S  E  L
  T  C  S  X  B  H  E  X  G  O  D  I  W
F  H  E  H  A  S  I  G  O  R  R  G  E  U  D
  J  S  L  R  L  P  B  A  D  C  Y  S  P
     T  Y  E  I  L  E  L  J  U  H  R
        B  M  P  S  R  B  E  T  A
           U  A  L  T  X  I  Y
              P  H  A  A  E
                 Y  F  R
                    U
```

Belief	Church	Faith	Lord
Bible	Comfort	God	Prayer
Christ	Cross	Jesus	Worship

Parable Puzzle

Sometimes, Jesus told stories called parables to teach his message. Fill in the missing letters to say which parable this picture is from.

In this parable, the woman hunted for her l _ _ _ c _ _ _.

Pieces Of Silver

These piles of silver coins all look the same, but one is different from the others. Can you spot which one it is?

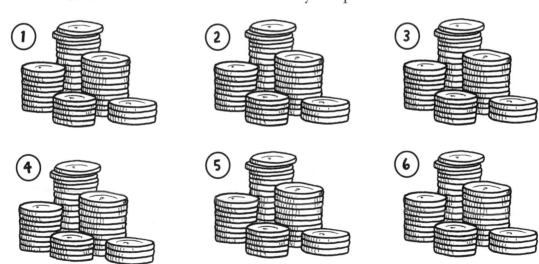

Lost Treasure

Which way did the woman go to find her lost coin?

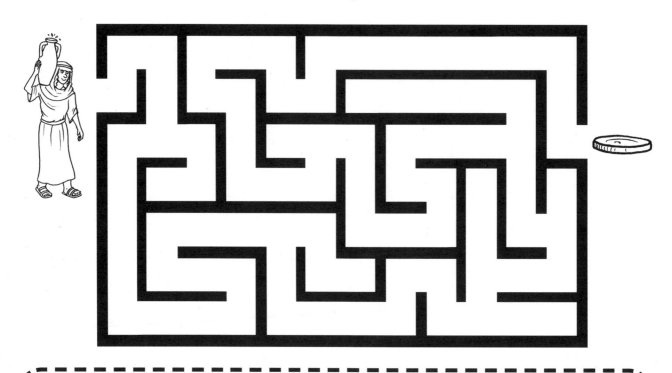

Words Of Wisdom

Look carefully at these word jumbles. Can you put each set of letters in the right order to spell out words from the New Testament?

1. DHRHPEES   ....

2. ORNESM   ....

3. LABREAP   ....

4. EARTHCE   ....

5. SPLIDCIE   ....

6. CIEALRM   ....

The Sermon On The Mount

The most important lessons that Jesus taught were given in speeches to the crowds from a hilltop. Use your pens or pencils to colour in this picture of Jesus giving his most famous sermon.

Hidden Books

Can you find these books from the New Testament hidden in this wordsearch?
The words read forwards, backwards, up, down and diagonally.

```
J  S  E  M  A  J  K  V  C  Z  Z  K  I  J
I  T  S  O  G  A  L  A  T  I  A  N  S  O
H  I  N  S  M  A  R  K  M  W  W  W  B  M
F  T  A  N  U  L  C  P  Q  Y  M  G  V  H
D  U  I  A  C  T  S  A  Y  V  A  V  R  O
U  S  H  I  R  E  V  E  L  A  T  I  O  N
H  V  T  S  L  U  K  E  Q  I  T  L  C  T
N  F  N  S  J  U  D  E  M  P  H  A  H  S
Z  M  I  O  T  X  X  O  A  V  E  U  L  Q
Y  I  R  L  T  C  T  M  J  R  W  L  U  V
K  J  O  O  O  H  D  Z  L  Y  B  C  H  E
Q  Q  C  C  Y  T  S  N  A  M  O  R  S  F
E  P  H  E  S  I  A  N  S  Z  R  J  Y  S
T  V  B  H  H  N  H  O  J  S  H  G  E  Q
```

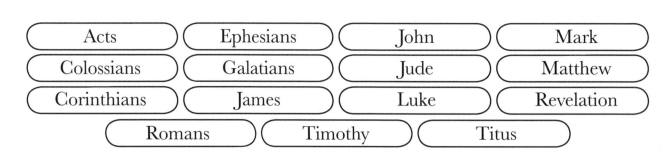

Acts	Ephesians	John	Mark
Colossians	Galatians	Jude	Matthew
Corinthians	James	Luke	Revelation
Romans	Timothy	Titus	

Lost And Found

Jesus told another parable about the joy of finding something important. Look at the picture and complete the sentence to reveal what this parable is about.

The S _ _ _ _ _ _ _ _ didn't give up until he found his lost s _ _ _ _ .

Holy Places

Fill in the missing letters to complete these biblical place names.

1. Na _ ar _ t _

2. B _ th _ eh _ m

3. Je _ u _ ale _

4. _ er _ co

5. E _ e _

6. Ga _ i _ e _

A Good Shepherd

Jesus was showing that it is more important to rescue a lost sheep than to watch over a flock that is already safe – and it's just the same with people! Which piece completes this picture of the shepherd?

Stray Sheep

Which way did the shepherd go to rescue the
stray sheep and bring it back to the flock?

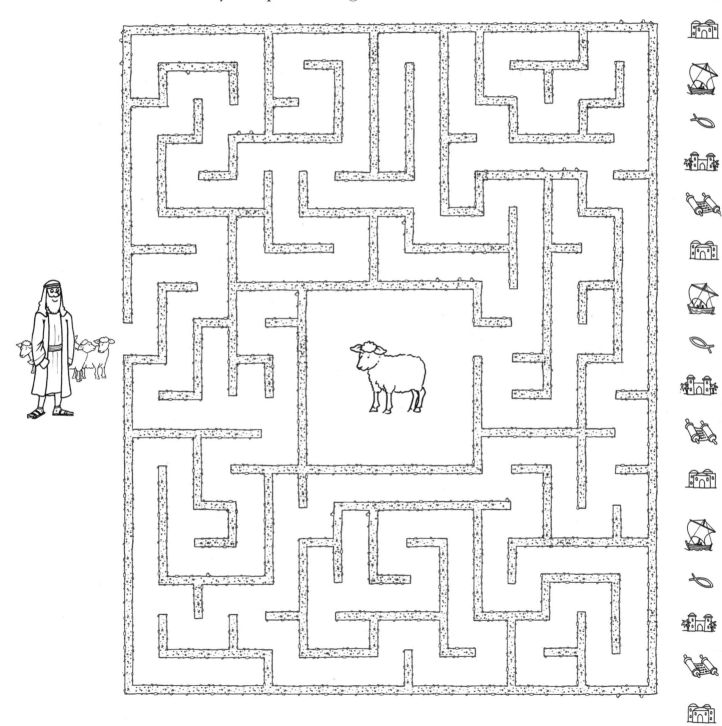

The Good Samaritan

One of Jesus' parables was about the time people passed by on the other side when robbers left a man injured in the road. How many crosses can you find hidden in this picture of a Samaritan stopping to help?

Kind Stranger

The Samaritan cleaned the man's wounds before paying for him to stay at a nearby inn. Can you spot the eight differences between these two pictures?

Samaritan Search

Can you find these words from the story of the Good Samaritan hidden in this wordsearch? They read forwards, backwards, up, down and diagonally.

```
F  M  I  G  M  H  I  Y  H  T  A  P  M  Y  S
L  F  G  S  H  X  K  B  O  N  R  O  C  J  Q
Y  H  N  V  G  P  Y  X  A  N  R  Q  O  C  I
S  J  O  T  E  N  T  T  L  O  A  D  N  M  H
N  L  R  I  Z  Y  I  H  U  I  R  E  C  G  M
F  J  E  A  D  R  K  H  N  S  O  Y  E  G  S
O  H  D  R  A  I  O  E  C  S  B  A  R  O  E
R  P  P  M  E  T  I  A  O  A  B  L  N  B  V
L  B  A  V  P  G  C  H  D  P  E  B  X  G  E
V  S  I  M  H  N  N  H  E  M  R  T  L  K  I
D  E  D  B  E  M  U  A  S  O  S  R  S  M  H
E  R  O  E  T  R  C  T  R  C  P  L  E  H  T
Z  U  D  Y  J  R  C  A  P  T  G  H  N  G  H
R  Y  T  Q  Y  L  Z  Y  Q  I  S  B  R  L  L
U  D  F  Y  P  A  R  A  B  L  E  Q  J  E  G
```

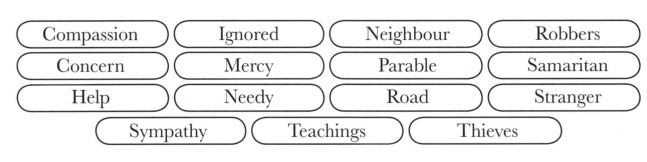

Compassion   Ignored   Neighbour   Robbers

Concern   Mercy   Parable   Samaritan

Help   Needy   Road   Stranger

Sympathy   Teachings   Thieves

God's House

These churches all look the same, but can you spot which one is different from the rest?

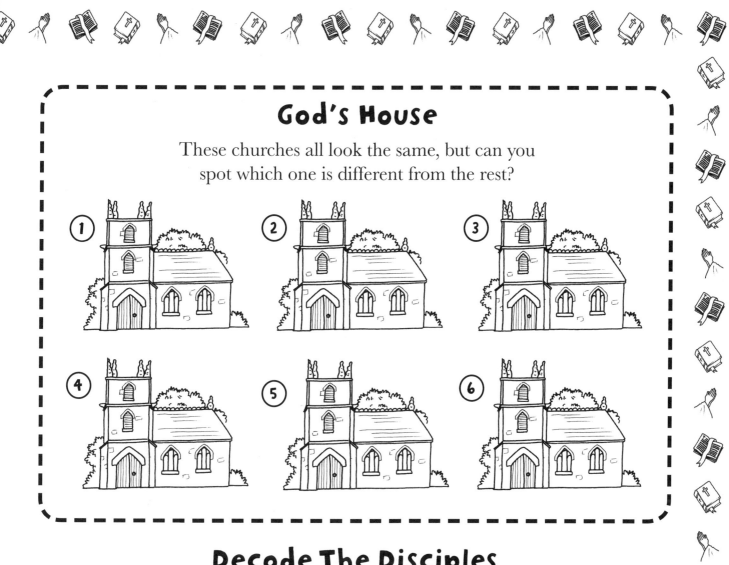

Decode The Disciples

Look carefully at these word jumbles. Can you put each set of letters in the right order to spell out the names of six disciples?

1. IPIHPL   ………………..

2. TWHTMAE   ………………..

3. SMJAE   ………………..

4. MOTHSA   ………………..

5. DSUJA   ………………..

6. MIOSN   ………………..

Healing Hands

On the way to Jerusalem, Jesus came across a group of ten very sick men who asked him to help them. Which piece completes this picture?

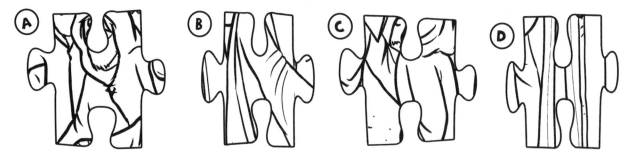

Cured At Last

Jesus took pity on the men and healed them all. Use your pencils or pens to colour the picture using the key below.

(1) Red (2) Green (3) Brown

(4) Blue (5) Yellow (6) Orange

Giving Thanks

Jesus healed ten sick people, but only one wanted to say thank you.
Which way did the man go to reach Jesus and show his gratitude?

Leaving Home

The parable known as The Prodigal Son tells of a young man
who left home with his father's money and wasted it all. Colour in
this picture of him leaving his family behind.

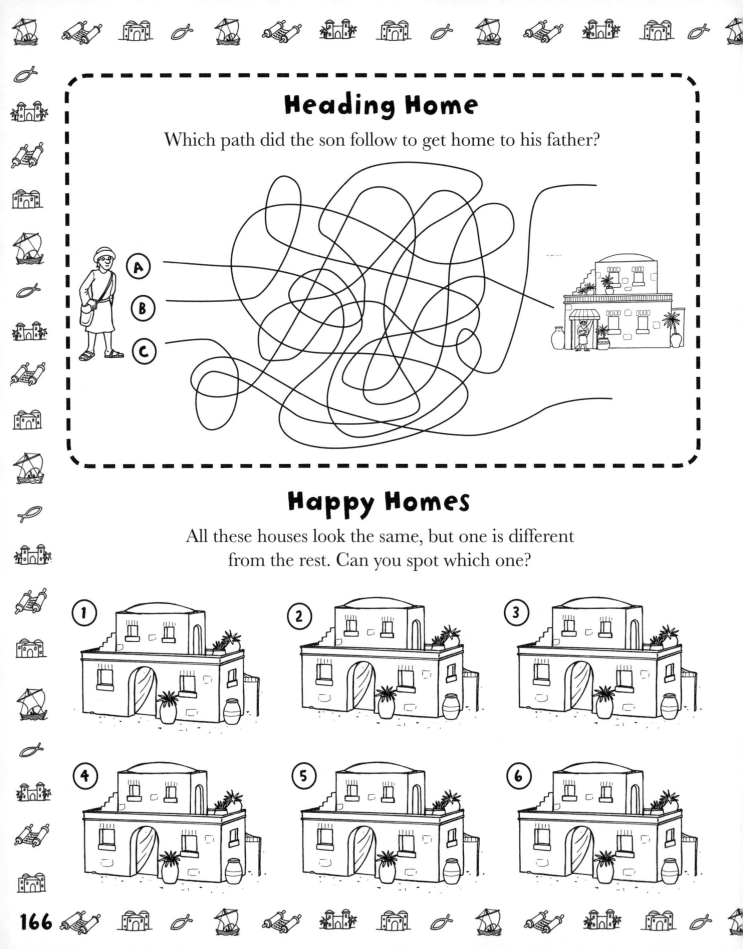

Heading Home

Which path did the son follow to get home to his father?

Happy Homes

All these houses look the same, but one is different from the rest. Can you spot which one?

A Warm Welcome

Even though the Prodigal Son had done something wrong, his father showed forgiveness and welcomed him home. Look carefully at this picture for 20 seconds and then turn the page to answer the questions without peeking back at it.

Question Time

Now you've studied the picture on page 167,
answer these questions about it from memory.

1. How many pointed trees are there in the picture?

2. What is the pattern on the curtains?

3. How many apples are there on the tree?

4. What is the man in the doorway holding?

5. How many flowers are growing in the garden?

6. What does the Prodigal Son have in his right hand?

7. How many windows does the house have?

Bonus question: Who didn't forgive the prodigal son?
a) His mother.   b) His cousin.   c) His brother.

Old Or New?

Do you know which testament each of these books is from?
Write 'old' or 'new' next to each one.

1. Acts   ....

2. Ezra   ....

3. Esther   ....

4. Revelation   ....

5. Psalms   ....

6. Hebrews   ....

Treetop Seat

Zacchaeus was a rich tax collector who wanted to see what Jesus looked like. Can you spot eight differences between these two pictures of him escaping the crowds by sitting in a tree?

Singled Out

Jesus spotted the man in the tree and asked to stay at his house. Colour in this picture of Jesus talking to Zacchaeus.

Tree Walk

Which way did Jesus walk to reach the tree that Zacchaeus was sitting in?

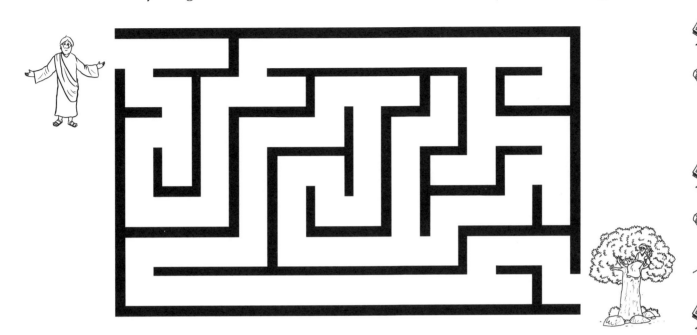

A New Man

After meeting Jesus, Zacchaeus changed his greedy ways.
Which of these pictures is different from the rest?

Reaching Jerusalem

Excited crowds cheered and waved palm branches when Jesus rode into
Jerusalem on a donkey. How many palm leaves can you count in this picture?
Once you've found them all, colour it in.

Sing Hosanna

The people of Jerusalem shouted 'Hosanna!' to show their love for Jesus.
Use your pencils or pens to colour the picture using the key below.

① Red ② Green ③ Brown ④ Blue
⑤ Yellow ⑥ Orange ⑦ Pink

Palm Sunday Search

Can you find these words from the Palm Sunday story hidden in this wordsearch? The words read forwards, backwards, up, down and diagonally.

```
U Q H C D        N T G S X
S Z B R F        O G N K J
D G S O O        I W I R E
O N D W L        S E T E R
N I N D L        S L E J U
K R E S O        E C E O S
E E I D W        C O R I A
Y E R P E        O M G C L
F H F U R        R E Q E E
U C L V S        P D C E M
                 Y G N I K
                 D M X I G
```

Cheering	Followers	Jerusalem
Crowds	Friends	King
Donkey	Greeting	Procession

Rejoice	Welcome

Jerusalem Journey

Which way did Jesus go to reach his followers in Jerusalem?

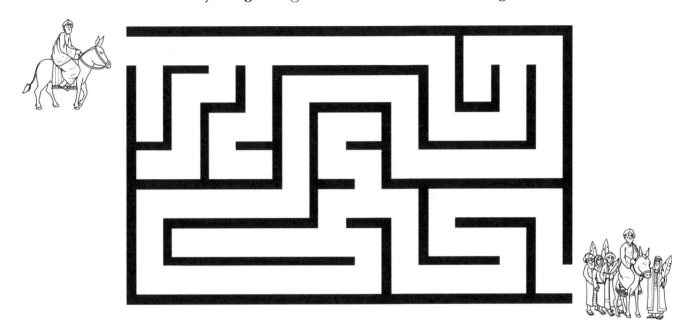

New Men

Fill in the missing letters to complete these names of men from the New Testament.

1. Ba _ th _ lo _ e _

2. G _ _ d S _ ma _ i _ an

3. P _ o _ ig _ l S _ n

4. S _ m _ n

5. Z _ c _ ha _ u _

6. _ ho _ a _

The Last Supper

Jesus predicted that his time on Earth was soon going to end, so he gathered his disciples for a special passover meal. Colour in this picture of the Last Supper.

Traitor At The Table

During the meal, Jesus announced that one of the disciples would betray him. Look carefully at this picture for 20 seconds and then turn the page to answer the questions from memory.

Table Test

Now you've studied the picture of the Last Supper on page 177, see if you can answer these questions without peeking back at it.

1. How many jugs are there in front of the table?
2. What is Jesus holding in his right hand?
3. How many oranges are there in the picture?
4. Is the door of the room open or closed?
5. How many windows are there?
6. What is the disciple on the left of Jesus holding?
7. How many wine glasses are in the picture?

Bonus question: Which part of the disciples' bodies did Jesus wash?
a) Their feet.   b) Their hands.   c) Their faces.

New Books

Fill in the missing letters to complete these books from the New Testament.

1. Re _ el _ ti _ n

2. P _ il _ m _ n

3. _ al _ ti _ n _

4. E _ he _ si _ ns

5. Co _ in _ hi _ ns

6. T _ es _ alo _ ia _ s

The Last Days

Jesus died on a cross to save mankind from their sins. Can you find the words from the crucifixion story hidden in this wordsearch?

```
H  B  I  W  T  N  E  M  H  S  I  N  U  P  N
U  P  O  N  T  I  U  S  P  I  L  A  T  E  R
B  C  G  F  E  T  R  Z  S  Q  T  F  S  A  Q
R  M  M  B  O  S  L  N  W  O  S  P  S  T  H
U  D  E  K  X  R  H  D  J  Q  R  D  I  T  E
H  H  S  Y  Y  N  G  E  A  Y  P  C  K  Y  A
F  X  S  N  O  I  X  I  F  I  C  U  R  C  O
Y  R  I  G  B  E  C  O  V  M  X  R  D  I  S
V  O  A  A  R  R  E  S  T  E  D  F  V  U  A
A  T  H  L  T  N  E  C  O  N  N  I  D  M  D
A  I  D  E  Y  A  R  T  E  B  B  E  U  A  U
R  A  D  R  D  S  O  L  D  I  E  R  S  R  J
M  R  S  E  L  P  I  C  S  I  D  X  H  S  V
A  T  J  E  S  U  S  C  H  R  I  S  T  V  G
C  P  X  R  A  O  C  R  U  A  E  L  K  F  N
```

Arrested	Crucifixion	Innocent	Kiss
Betrayed	Disciples	Jesus Christ	Messiah
Cross	Forgiveness	Judas	Pontius Pilate
	Punishment	Soldiers	Traitor

Jesus Lives

The heavy stone in front of the tomb where Jesus was buried had been moved aside when some women went to visit the grave. Jesus had been resurrected! Use your favourite pens and pencils to colour in this joyful picture.

ANSWERS

ANSWERS

5. God's Busy Week

7. Which World?

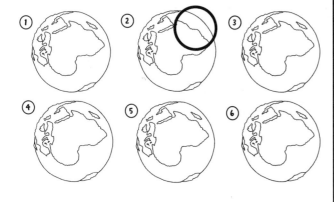

7. Wonderful Work

1. Light and darkness 2. Sky 3. Land and sea
4. Sun, moon and stars 5. Birds and sea
creatures 6. Animals and humans
7. God rested

8. One World

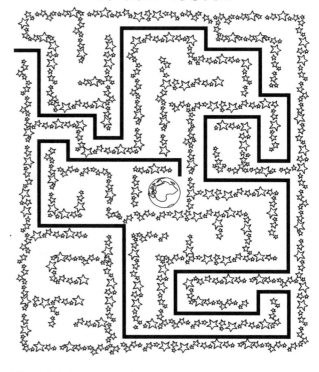

9. Creation Search

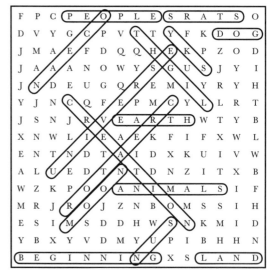

ANSWERS

10. Adam And Eve

12. The Garden Of Eden

1. A snake 2. Eve 3. Eve
4. There are 10 apples on the tree
5. There are 8 leaves on the tree
6. There are 19 flowers 7. Adam

Bonus question: b) Eden

12. Forbidden Fruit

Line C leads to the apple tree

13. Temptation Wordsearch

14. Slippery Serpent

14. Leafy Letters

You could have had: endangered, deafened, defender, renegade, angered, groaned, adored, agreed, danger, degree, dodger, dragon, eroded, garden, geared, needed, orange, eager, faded, grade, grand, greed, green, groan, frog, gone, rang, read, road, age, ago, and, dog, ear, odd, one, rag, ran, do, go, of, on, or

15. Flood Alert

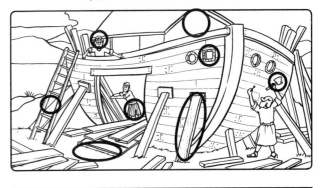

16. Water World

Piece C is the missing part of the puzzle

ANSWERS

18. Knowing Noah

1. Three. 2. Four. 3. Ten 4. Monkey
5. A carrot 6. Giraffe 7. Elephants

Bonus question:

b) Forty days and forty nights

---

18. Land Ahoy!

Path A leads to the tree

---

19. On Dry Land

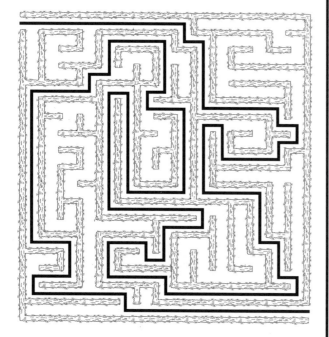

20. Looking For Land

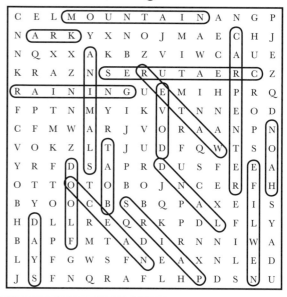

---

21. What's The Story?

The missing words are: Tower, Babel

---

21. Tower Tour

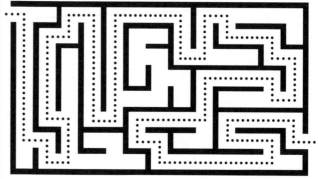

ANSWERS

22. Men At Work

23. Tower Tools

24. Sky Scraper

Piece D is the missing part of the puzzle

26. Which Way To Canaan?

Path C leads to Canaan

26. Hush Little Baby

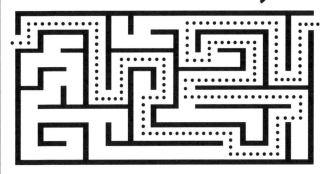

27. A New Baby

Piece B is the missing part of the puzzle

29. Eyes On Isaac

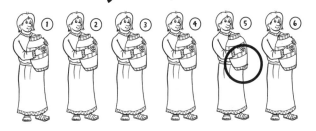

29. Abraham's Test

1. Abraham, sacrifices 2. God, loyal
3. Isaac 4. three, mountain 5. angel, test

30. Isaac And Rebekah

Piece A is the missing part of the puzzle

ANSWERS

31. Marriage Maze

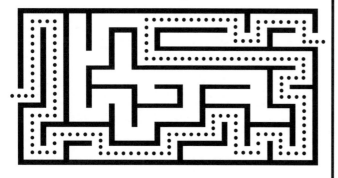

31. Well, Well!

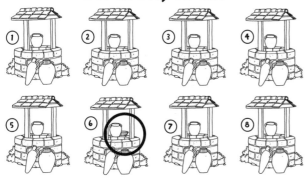

32. Jacob's Dream

The missing words are: ladder, heaven

32. Awesome Angels

Angel C is about to travel up the ladder to heaven

34. Lucky Joseph

36. The Story Of Joseph

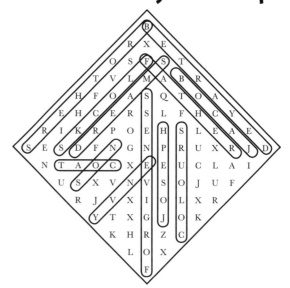

ANSWERS

37. Envious Brothers

Piece C is the missing part of the puzzle

39. Off To Egypt

Brother A did a deal with the trader

39. Brotherly Love

1. Reuben 2. Simeon 3. Levi 4. Judah
5. Issachar 6. Zebulun 7. Benjamin 8. Dan
9. Naphtali 10. Gad 11. Asher

40. Hard Work

Piece A is the missing part of the puzzle

42. River Bed

43. Furious Pharaoh

You could have had: realities, serialise, earliest,
realises, realise, serials, teasers, alerts, easier,
easter, erases, lasers, litres, raises, series, sister,
stairs, steals, steers, teases, trails, trials, aisle,
alert, lasts, later, least, liars, rails, raise, stale,
stare, stars, steal, tails, tears, tiles, east, eats, art,
let, lie, see, sir, as, at, is, it

43. Moses Baskets

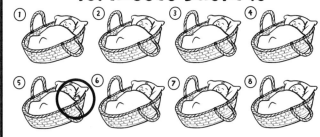

45. Finding Moses

46. The Second Plague

Piece A is the missing part of the puzzle

48. Plague Picture

1. Four 2. At the foot of the tree 3. Four
4. A bucket 5. An eye
6. A donkey and a cow 7. One

Bonus question: b) Insects

ANSWERS

48. Jumping Frogs

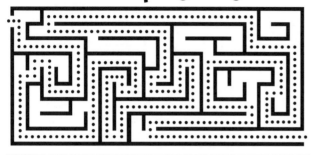

49. The Passover

There are 13 brushes

50. Freedom Food

52. Moses Memory Game

1. Three 2. A child 3 Three
4 A stick/staff 5. Five 6. Three 7. Open

Bonus question:

c) Moses parted the waves

52. A Friend In The Flames

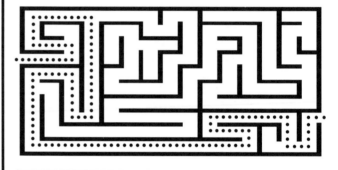

54. Finding Freedom

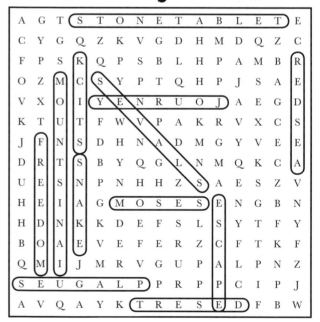

ANSWERS

56. Moses Maze

57. Manna From Heaven

Piece B is the missing part of the puzzle

58. Missing Moses

1. Pharaoh 2. ten 3. Israelites 4. army
5. Red Sea 6. manna 7. Mount Sinai

58. Holy Food

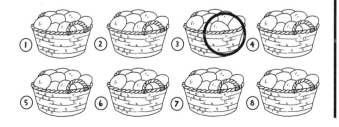

60. Messenger Moses

There are ten small stone tablets

62. Commandments Questions

1. One 2. Stone tablets showing the Ten
Commandments 3. Three 4. Nothing
5. Eight 6. VI 7. None

Bonus question: b) Sinai

62. Mountain Path

Moses followed path C

64. Commandments Quiz

1. gods 2. idols 3. honour 4. Sabbath
5. father, mother 6. murder 7. adultery
8. steal 9. false witness 10. covet

ANSWERS

64. The Golden Calf

65. Moab Bound

Piece A is the missing part of the puzzle

66. Angel Crossing

The missing words are: donkey, angel

66. A Talking Donkey

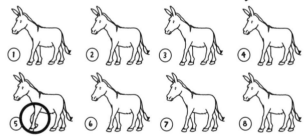

67. Tumbling Walls

Soldier B caused the wall to fall

67. Missing Joshua

1. Joshua, Jericho 2. march, six 3. city, day
4. seventh, seven 5. sounded, horns
6. blew, shouted

70. Samson's Strength

1. Four 2. An X 3. Three 4. Running away
5. Two 6. Square 7. Four

Bonus question: a) Delilah

70. Spot Samson

71. Samson's Secret

ANSWERS

72. Devious Delilah

73. Samson Search

74. Special Places

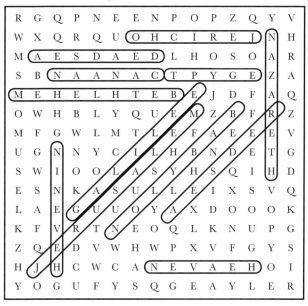

76. Remember Ruth

1. Four 2. Twelve 3. Ten 4. Four
5. A water jug 6. Six
7. A bundle of wheat/grain

Bonus question:

b) Her mother-in-law

76. Fields Of Gold

Path C leads to the field of grain

77. Kind Boaz

Piece A is the missing part of the puzzle

ANSWERS

78. Hannah's Prayer

There are 10 flowers

79. Special Son

80. People Of The Bible

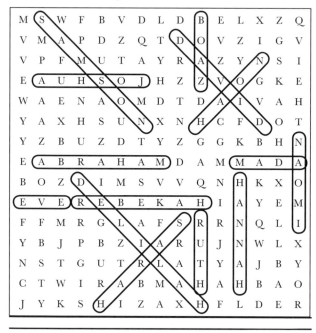

81. A New King

The missing words are: David, Israel

81. Harp Harmony

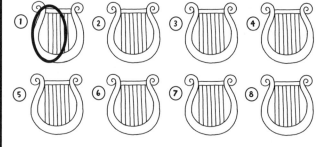

ANSWERS

83. David vs Goliath

84. Sling Search

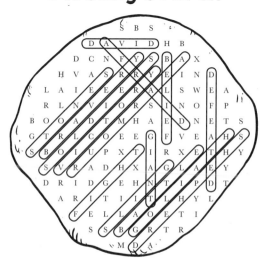

86. Question Time

1. Ten 2. Two swords 3. Two 4. A sling
5. Four 6. A stone 7. Eight

Bonus question: b) A shepherd boy

86. Home Sweet Home

1. C 2. E 3. B 4. D 5. A

87. Champion Israelite

88. A Royal Visit

You could have had: measure, measle, erase, laser, mules, mural, arms, ears, eels, emus, mars, meal, sale, same, seal, seam, slam, slum, sure, user, ale, are, arm, jam, jar, ram, sea, see, sum, use, am, as, me, us

88. Kind Queen

ANSWERS

90. Guidance From God

There are 11 crowns

91. The First Temple

Piece B is the missing part of the puzzle

92. Healing Naaman

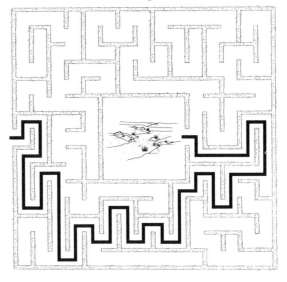

93. River Miracle

Piece C is the missing part of the puzzle

94. Jonah's Lesson

You could have had: hurricane, richer, urchin, chain, chair, china, churn, crane, crier, curer, care, chin, cure, each, earn, hair, hare, hear, hire, inch, near, nice, race, rain, rare, rice, rich, ruin, ace, air, can, car, cue, her, run, urn, an, he

94. Find The Fishing Boat

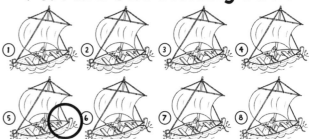

ANSWERS

96. Jonah's Memory Game

1. Two 2. Octopus 3. One 4. Spots
5. 23 6. Open 7. Four

Bonus question: b) Nineveh

96. Whale Tangle

Line B leads to the whale

97. There She Blows!

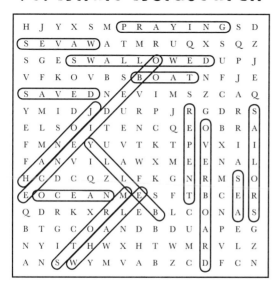

98. Whale Wordsearch

100. Writing On The Wall

Piece C is the missing part of the puzzle

101. Belshazzar's Search

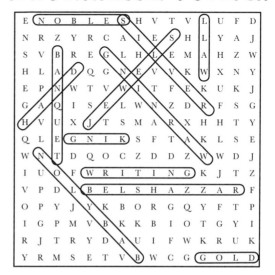

102. Daniel And The Lions

There are 9 candles

ANSWERS

103. Daniel's Prayer

105. Daniel's Wordsearch

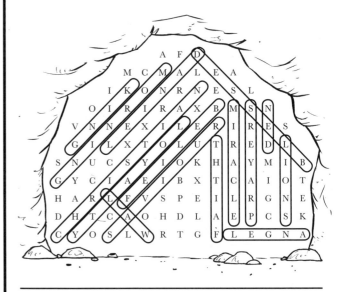

104. Lion Look-a-likes

108. City Saviour

You could have had: meanie, anime, ahem, amen, main, mane, mean, mine, name, aim, ham, hem, hen, him, man, men, nah, am, an, eh, ha, he, hi, in, ma, me

104. Angel Tangle

Angel C looked after Daniel

108. Journey To Jerusalem

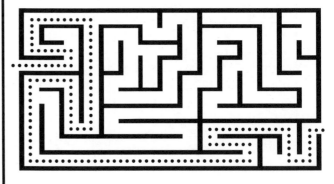

ANSWERS

109. Psalms Search

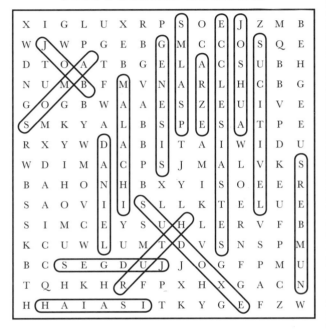

112. Mary's Memory Game

1. Four 2. Flowers 3. Three 4. Apples
5. Broom 6. Flowers 7. A rope

Bonus question:

c) That she would have a baby son called Jesus

112. Angel Assembly

113. Joseph The Carpenter

Piece B is the missing part of the puzzle

114. Happy Couple

115. Guardian Angels

There are 10 angels

ANSWERS

116. Busy Bethlehem

117. A Child Is Born

The missing words are: Jesus, manger

117. A Place To Stay

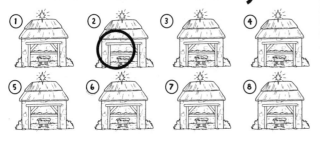

119. Night Light

120. While Shepherds Watched

Shepherd C needs to turn back

120. Nativity Names

1. Joseph 2. Donkey 3. Jesus
4. Shepherds 5. Mary 6. Bethlehem

121. We Three Kings

Piece A is the missing part of the puzzle

122. Nativity Wordsearch

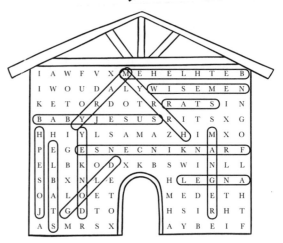

ANSWERS

124. Memory Game

1. Nine 2. A goblet 3. Six 4. A star
5. Three 6. Grapes 7. Two

Bonus question: a) Herod

124. Eastern Treasures

125. Herod's Anger

Piece C is the missing part of the puzzle

126. Fleeing Herod

Line D leads them to the donkey

126. Oh, Little Town

You could have had: beetle, helmet, melee,
theme, belt, beth, heel, helm, meet, melt, them,
bee, bet, eel, elm, hem, lee, let, met, tee, the,
be, he, me

127. Egypt Bound

128. Jesus Is Baptised

There are 10 goblets

ANSWERS

129. Just John

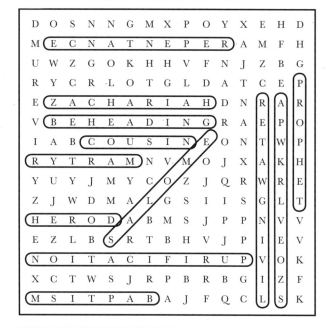

```
D O S N N G M X P O Y X E H D
M E C N A T N E P E R A M F H
U W Z G O K H H V F N J Z B G
R Y C R L O T G L D A T C E P
E Z A C H A R I A H D N R E R
V B E H E A D I N G R A A P O
I A B C O U S I N E O N T K P
R Y T R A M N V M O J X W R H
Y U Y J M Y C O Z J Q R W L E
Z J W D M A L G S I I S G V T
H E R O D A B M S J P P N I V
E Z L B S R T B H V J P I O V
N O I T A C I F I R U P V Z K
X C T W S J R P B R B G I S F
M S I T P A B A J F Q C L R K
```

131. Follow Me

133. God's Workers

Piece A is the missing part of the puzzle

134. Disciple Difference

134. Finding James

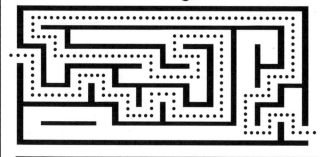

135. Name Game

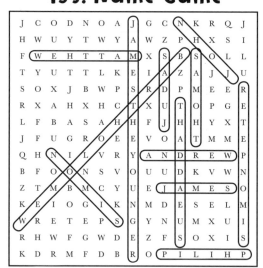

```
J C O D N O A J G C N K R Q J
H W U Y T W Y A W Z P H X S I
F W E H T T A M X S B S O L L
T Y U T T L K E I A Z A J J U
S O X J B W P S D P M E E R E
R X A H X H C T X U T O P G E
L F B A S A H H F J H Y X T E
J F U G R O E E V O A T M M E
Q H N I L V R Y A N D R E W N
B F O O N S V O U U D K V W N
Z T M B M C Y U E J A M E S O
K E I O G I K N M D E S E L M
W R E T E P S G Y N U M X U I
R H W F G W D E Z F S O X I S
K D R M F D B R O P I L I H P
```

ANSWERS

137. A Helping Hand

The missing words are: Mary, first

137. Water Or Wine?

Jar A was turned into wine

138. The Lord Knows

There are 10 buckets

140. Miracle Memory Game

1. Three 2. A loaf and a fish 3. Two
4. One 5. Three 6. Triangle
7. Seven

Bonus question:

c) Five loaves and two fishes

140. Packed Lunches

141. Loaves And Fishes

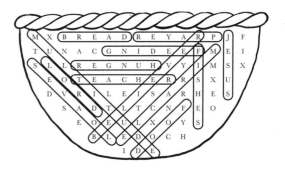

142. Picnic Of Plenty

ANSWERS

143. Truly Thankful

145. A Child In Need

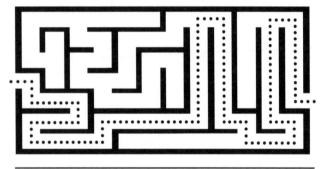

145. Story Time

1. Samson and Delilah
2. Moses and the Ten Commandments
3. Noah's Ark 4. The Twelve Disciples
5. John the Baptist 6. David and Goliath

147. Sudden Storm

Piece B is the missing part of the puzzle

148. A Good Catch

Fisherman C caught a full net of fish

148. Calming The Waters

You could have had: allege, agile, eagle, legal, gale, gall, gill, glee, age, ail, ale, all, eel, gee, gel, ill, lag, lee, leg, lie

150. Worship Wordsearch

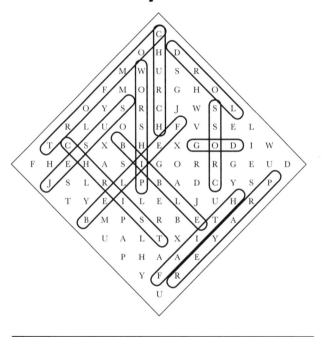

151. Parable Puzzle

The missing words are: lost, coin

ANSWERS

151. Pieces Of Silver

152. Lost Treasure

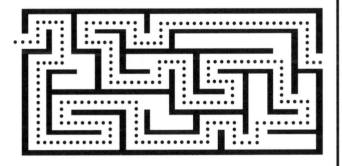

152. Words Of Wisdom

1. shepherd 2. sermon 3. parable
4. teacher 5. disciple 6. miracle

154. Hidden Books

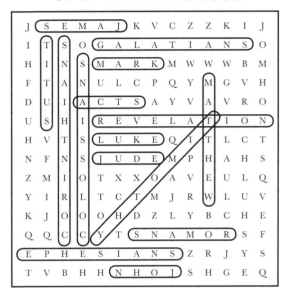

155. Holy Places

1. Nazareth 2. Bethlehem 3. Jerusalem
4. Jericho 5. Eden 6. Galilee

155. Lost And Found

The missing words are: Shepherd, sheep

156. A Good Shepherd

Piece D completes the puzzle

ANSWERS

157. Stray Sheep

159. Kind Stranger

160. Samaritan Search

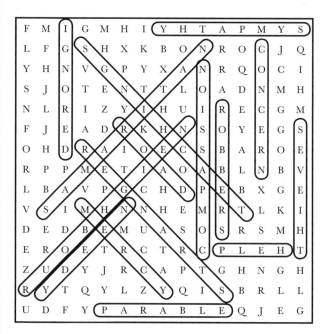

158. The Good Samaritan

There are 10 crosses

ANSWERS

161. God's House

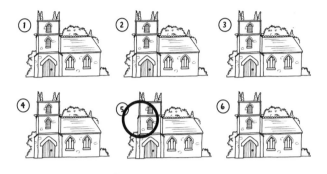

161. Decode The Disciples

1. Philip 2. Matthew 3. James
4. Thomas 5. Judas 6. Simon

162. Healing Hands

Piece A is the missing part of the puzzle

164. Giving Thanks

166. Heading Home

The son followed path B to get home

166. Happy Homes

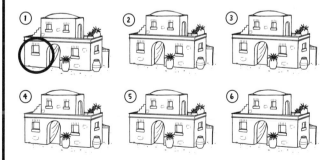

ANSWERS

168. Question Time

1. Four 2. Spots and stripes
3. Five 4. A broom 5. Six
6. Walking stick 7. Two

Bonus question: c) His brother

---

168. Old Or New?

1. New Testament 2. Old Testament
3. Old Testament 4. New Testament
5. Old Testament 6. New Testament

---

169. Treetop Seat

---

171. Tree Walk

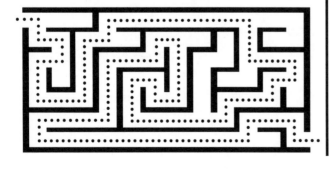

171. A New Man

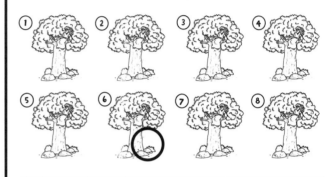

---

172. Reaching Jerusalem

There are 16 palm leaves

ANSWERS

174. Palm Sunday Search

175. Jerusalem Journey

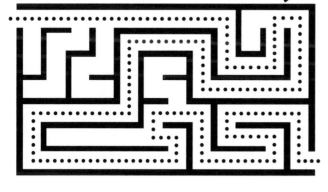

175. New Men

1. Bartholomew 2. Good Samaritan
3. Prodigal Son 4. Simon
5. Zacchaeus 6. Thomas

178. Table Test

1. Three 2. A goblet 3. Five 4. Closed
5. Two 6. A loaf of bread 7. Five

Bonus question: a) Their feet

178. New Books

1. Revelation 2. Philemon 3. Galatians
4. Ephesians 5. Corinthians 6. Thessalonians

179. The Last Days

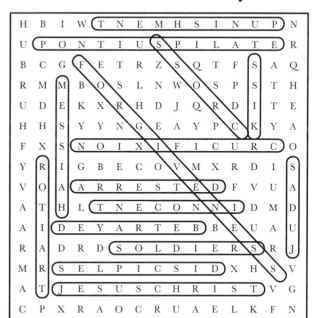